Natchez Under-the-HIll

A sequel to
The Devil's Highway

Stan Applegate

Illustrated by
James Watling

℗
JR

A Peachtree Junior Publication

Published by
PEACHTREE PUBLISHERS, LTD.
494 Armour Circle NE
Atlanta, Georgia 30324

www.peachtree-online.com

Text © 1999 by Stanley Applegate
Cover and text illustrations © 1999 by James Watling

Book design by Loraine M. Balcsik
Composition by Melanie M. McMahon

Manufactured in the United States of America

10 9 8 7 6 5 4 3 2 1
First Edition

Library of Congress Cataloging-in-Publication Data

Applegate, Stanley.
　　Natchez Under-the-Hill / by Stanley Applegate ; illustrated by James Watling. –1st ed.
　　　　p. cm.
　　　Sequel to: The devil's highway.
　　　Summary: Fourteen-year-old Zeb survives skirmishes with horse thieves and other outlaws as he travels the dangerous Natchez Trace in 1811 while searching for his grandfather.
　　ISBN 1-56145-191-6
　　[1. Frontier and pioneer life—Fiction. 2. Natchez Trace—Fiction. 3. Grandfathers—Fiction.] I. Watling, James, ill. II. Title.
　　PZ7.A6487Nat 1999
　　[Fic]—dc 21
　　　　　　　　　　　　　　　　　　　　98-43051
　　　　　　　　　　　　　　　　　　　　CIP
　　　　　　　　　　　　　　　　　　　　AC

ACKNOWLEDGMENTS

I wish, once again, to thank Carol Lee Lorenzo and members of the Children's Writing Group at Emory University for all of their help and encouragement. I am also particularly grateful to Sherrie Jamison and her fifth- and sixth-grade students at Burghard Elementary School in Macon, Georgia, for their commentary on the manuscript.

I wish to thank Sarah Helyar Smith, my editor at Peachtree Publishers, who worked with me from the outset on the development of THE DEVIL'S HIGHWAY and the sequel, NATCHEZ UNDER-THE-HILL; Amy Sproull, Associate Editor at Peachtree Publishers, who helped me fine-tune NATCHEZ UNDER-THE-HILL; and my agent, Joan Brandt, for her criticism and good counsel.

For their assistance on historical research, I am deeply indebted to Mimi Miller, Director of Preservation and Education Director of the Historic Natchez Foundation, and to Barbara Potter, research associate of the foundation. Whenever there seemed to be no historical reference available, Mimi Miller suggested I talk with Mr. Elbert Hilliard, Director of the Mississippi Department of Archives and History. "If anyone knows, he will," she said. Mr. Hilliard has provided me with wonderful resources, among them "Horse Racing in the Old Natchez District 1783–1830," an article written by his predecessor and mentor, Laura D. S. Harrell, and published in the *Journal of Mississippi History* in July 1951. It proved invaluable in my efforts to make NATCHEZ UNDER-THE-HILL as historically accurate as possible.

I am also indebted to Meyers Brown of the Atlanta History Center and, although I have not met him, to Randy Steffin for his scholarship and his extraordinary illustrations in THE HORSE SOLDIER, 1776–1943 (Volumes I to IV, Norman: University of Oklahoma Press, 1977).

Table of
CONTENTS

CHAPTER ONE

Revenge

Washington, Mississippi Territory
October 13, 1811

Zeb awoke on a barn floor in front of a horse stall to find Hannah squatting next to him, poking him in the ribs. She was smiling, but her eyes were red and teary.

He jumped up, dusting the straw off his pants. "You all right?" he whispered.

She nodded and began to speak, but he interrupted her.

"How long was I asleep?" he whispered. "I've got to leave for Natchez right away...."

"You haven't been asleep long. I'm sorry I took a while to come back," Hannah said. "I shouldn't have left you to take care of the horses alone. But Mama and Father and I had so much to talk about.

She headed toward the door. "C'mon," she called. "My parents want to meet you."

As they neared the house, Hannah's mother hurried toward them. She wore a white cotton dress, drawn in at the waist and almost reaching her ankles. Her long black hair was pulled into a single braid down her back. She looked a lot like Hannah, with her fawn-colored skin and big brown eyes and with the same tall, erect way of walking.

Hannah almost skipped as she ran to her. She yelled to Zeb, "C'mon!"

How very young she seems now that she's home, he thought, *much younger than her eleven years. After six months with an outlaw gang, it's a wonder she can be so happy.*

He lifted his nose and smelled something wonderful cooking. He felt a rush of saliva in his mouth.

Hannah's mother reached out and took Zeb's hands in hers. She was smiling, but her eyes were red like Hannah's. "I want to apologize to you, Zebulon. We didn't mean to ignore you when you arrived. It was just such a shock, having Hannah home at last."

She stared at him. "You do look just like he said you would, but I expected someone much older, someone…different. You're just a boy."

Zeb stood as tall as he could. After more than a month on the Natchez Road, he no longer thought of himself as a boy. "I'm fourteen, ma'am. I'll be fifteen in March…." He frowned. "But who told you what I look like?"

Dr. McAllister sat on a bench on the wide back porch, his white lab coat hanging loosely on his shoulders. He got to his feet, pushing against the wall for support. He moved toward the porch rail.

"Zebulon, a man came here and told us that you had kidnapped Hannah, that you were a dangerous outlaw, armed to the teeth, tall and skinny, with a mop of shaggy hair. He said you were riding a big, funny-looking horse."

"Dangerous outlaw?" Zeb's voiced cracked. "A kidnapper? But who would—"

"Don't worry," Hannah's mother said, pulling Hannah against her. She smiled. "You don't need to explain. Hannah has told us all about you. We know you're not a kidnapper. We

2

know that, without you, Hannah would never have been able to get home."

"But who told you I was a kidnapper?"

Dr. McAllister leaned forward a bit unsteadily, his hands on the porch rail. "A man visited us here a few days ago," he said. "He told us that he had news of Hannah. We invited him in. He was a terrible man, huge, with greasy black hair, missing a couple of fingers on his right hand. He was wearing what looked to be an army uniform, but the insignia had been ripped off."

Hannah gasped. "The sergeant!"

Zeb nodded. "Must've passed us while we were at Yockanookany Village. Got a horse somehow."

Dr. McAllister called to them. "Please," he said, "come up to the porch. We can sit and talk."

Zeb shook his head as he climbed the porch steps. "I really need to be on my way, sir. I'll be leavin' here in a few minutes...." He looked back at the stable. "Would it be all right for me to leave the packhorse here while I go to Natchez to look for my grampa?"

"Of course," Dr. McAllister said. He shook Zeb's hand. "We want to thank you, Zebulon, for helping Hannah come home. She never would have made it without you."

Dr. McAllister pointed once again to the porch chair. "Please sit down, Zebulon. We have some important news for you.

"That sergeant," he continued, "told us that the kidnapper was headed this way with Hannah and that he had a plan to intercept them. He would rescue Hannah and see that the kidnapper got his just deserts. He wanted a large sum of money to rescue Hannah."

Hannah's mother interrupted. "We were both ready to pay whatever he asked. But he wanted the money in advance. I didn't trust him, so we told him that we would pay him if he delivered Hannah."

Dr. McAllister nodded. "He was furious. He said when he found Hannah, we'd have to pay double what he was asking."

The doctor put his hand on Zeb's shoulder. "The sergeant will be a serious problem for you. He swore he was going to get you, if it was the last thing he ever did. I'm sure he's in Natchez—or more likely, down in Natchez Under-the-Hill—waiting for you. You'll need to be very careful."

Zeb looked up as a black woman came out of the kitchen and onto the porch. "Miz Martha," she said, "I'll have the noon meal ready in about an hour."

She paused, looking down at Hannah. "I have hot water on the stove, and I can have that tub filled in a minute."

Then she looked at Zeb. "And I can heat more water, just in case anybody else feels the need for a bath."

Zeb was suddenly aware of the sour, sweaty odor of his and Hannah's unwashed clothes. They had been traveling a week since Yockanookany, too anxious to keep moving to stop and wash clothes and bathe.

Hannah's mother put her arm around Hannah. "Let's go get you cleaned up." The two of them walked into the house.

Zeb thought about his mama. He remembered her comforting arm around his shoulders after his daddy died. He sighed.

Dr. McAllister leaned back against the wall. "I'll never be able to thank you enough," he said.

Sarah was singing in the kitchen. Dr. McAllister smiled. "Sarah really loves Hannah. For seven long months she was sure Hannah was still alive."

Dr. McAllister glanced toward the kitchen. "Sarah was with me for fifteen years before I married Martha. I wasn't sure she would take to a new family."

4

"That must be difficult for a slave...."

Dr. McAllister turned to him and said in a low, measured voice, "Sarah is no slave. I would never have a slave. She was manumitted as a child...you know, given her freedom. The owner died and willed all of his slaves to be freed. Her husband was freed as an adult. He works as a blacksmith here in town."

Dr. McAllister paused. "I know that you want to leave right away to look for your grandfather," he said. "But wouldn't it be better to rest here for an hour or two, have a bath, and change into clean clothes? You'll want to be presentable so people in Natchez will speak to you. We can have our midday meal and then you can be on your way."

Zeb knew that what Dr. McAllister was suggesting was the best thing. It was just that he was now only an hour or so from Natchez, and he had spent more than a month trying to get there to find his grampa. He felt like jumping on Christmas and galloping into the city to start searching. But Christmas didn't have much gallop left in him, and Zeb had to admit that he, too, was very tired.

"Thank you, sir," he said. "A few hours' rest would be a good idea." He wrinkled his nose. "And I sure could use a bath."

"Your horse has been traveling for more than a month, sometimes carrying two riders," Dr. McAllister pointed out. "If you're determined to go today, why don't you take Hannah's horse, Suba?"

Zeb shook his head. "But Hannah—"

Dr. McAllister smiled. "Don't worry, it was Hannah's idea. The horse is very high-strung. Not everyone can ride her, but Hannah is sure that you can. She uses a light English saddle on Suba. It's almost a racing saddle. She says it's like riding bareback."

Zeb nodded. "You're right. The horses are exhausted. I'd love to ride Suba into Natchez.... But could she carry two?"

"She's very strong. I'm sure she could carry both you and your grandfather for a short distance."

"You said 'racing saddle'? Has Suba raced?"

"Not yet. But I'm sure she would do well."

Zeb got up and started to pace. "I'm sorry," he said, "I just can't sit anymore." He flexed his knees. "So I guess Suba hasn't been ridden much with Hannah away."

"We keep her at Culpepper's farm where she can run. They exercise her every day." Dr. McAllister looked up at Zeb. "Even so, she might be a real handful."

"I'd sure like to find out."

Dr. McAllister smiled. "Did Hannah tell you why she calls her horse Suba?"

Zeb nodded. "She said the horse's name is Isuba Lusa, Choctaw for Black Horse."

"That's right. Hannah was only six years old when she got the horse, and just called her Suba."

Dr. McAllister looked down at Zeb's feet. "You'll never be able to ride Suba wearing those Choctaw moccasins. I've got an old pair of boots you can borrow. I think we're about the same size."

"Thank you, sir. I'd appreciate it."

Zeb smelled fresh bread just out of the oven and chicken roasted with some spices he couldn't identify. *I'm so hungry! It'll be strange to eat at a table again.* He closed his eyes, remembering the smells of his mama's cooking.

Dr. McAllister leaned back against the wall, studying Zeb.

"Hannah told us about Tate McPhee's men. There were two of them right behind you that first day on the Natchez Road?"

Zeb nodded.

"It's more than likely they followed you all the way to Natchez. And McPhee may be with them."

"I hope to find Grampa before McPhee gets here."

6

"He may already be here. You spent several days at Yockanookany Village—they could have passed you. You'll have to take great care when looking for your grampa so they won't find out where he is."

"I'll be careful. He's sure to be around Natchez, if he's still alive. I'll check at King's Tavern first. He always stayed there and used that as his address for anyone tryin' to sell or buy horses. He told me that the post rider always stops there."

They sat together on the bench, each in his own thoughts.

Zeb lifted his head as Sarah stepped out on the porch, still humming. "I thought I'd fix up that little back room for Master Zebulon here," she offered.

"I'd sure appreciate havin' a place to stay," Zeb said. "I may not need it tonight, though. If I'm not back by dark, I'll be stayin' in Natchez at King's Tavern."

Dr. McAllister shook his head. "I doubt you'll find a place to stay this week, with the cotton buyers in town."

He eased his back away from the wall. "I'll draw you a little map of Natchez to help you get around. It's not difficult. King's Tavern is right on the road from here to Natchez, just inside the city limits."

Dr. McAllister turned to Zeb. "One more thing," he said. "Tomorrow morning, we'll come into Natchez to see if we can be of any help to you. Leave us a message at King's Tavern to let us know where we can find you."

"You don't need to go to all of that trouble. I'll be all right."

"No," Dr. McAllister said, "we'll be there. I don't do much riding anymore, and as you must have seen, those old horses in the barn aren't much. But Natchez isn't very far. We may be able to help you find your grandfather, and I want to talk with the police constable about Tate McPhee and the sergeant."

CHAPTER TWO

The Culpeppers

October 13, 1811

Dr. McAllister and Zeb turned as they heard the front gate squeak open. Nashoba and two Choctaw braves, clad in deerskin pants and shirts, led their horses around the house and into the backyard.

Nashoba handed his reins to one of the braves and ran up to the porch. He nodded to Zeb and shook Dr. McAllister's hand. "It is good to see you, sir."

"Good to see you, Nashoba. Hannah and her mother are upstairs. They'll be down in a minute. Please sit down."

"I'm sorry, sir. I won't be able to stay." Nashoba pointed to his companions. "The *nakni*, the braves, brought me a message from Yowani. My father is there, and he has been hurt. He had been visiting with the Creek Indians. I don't know the details. He wants to see me as soon as possible."

"But that's terrible, Nashoba. I wonder what happened? Even though he is a white man, he has always been accepted by the nations he has visited."

"I don't know. The nakni don't know. But I must go back immediately. I'll just wait to say good-bye to Hannah and her mother, then we'll be on our way north."

Hannah burst out of the door, followed by her mother.

Hannah was wearing one of the two sets of boy's clothes she had brought from Yowani. "Nashoba!" she cried. "Did I hear you say you hafta go back to Yowani?"

"My father is there. He's been badly hurt and he needs me."

"Oh, Nashoba," she said. "I'm so sorry. But thank you so much for helping us get down here from Yowani."

Hannah's mother took his hand in hers. "We thank you, too, Nashoba." She nodded to the two nakni. "I know you'll want to leave right away. I'll put together some food for you to take along." She hurried toward the kitchen.

Zeb called over his shoulder as he ran to the barn at the back of the yard. "We still have those deerskin food bags we got from the villagers at Yockanookany."

Hannah threw her arms around Nashoba's waist. "I'm gonna miss you, Nashoba. I hope we'll get back to Yowani soon."

He patted her short hair and hugged her. "I'm going to miss you, too, Hannah. I'm so glad that you're home and safe." Hannah stepped back and looked up at him.

Nashoba turned to Zeb. He held out his hand. "I'm proud to call you brother," he said. They shook hands and thumped each other on the back. Zeb, Nashoba, and the two nakni loaded the food into the bags.

Dr. McAllister took Nashoba's hand. "Thank you again, Nashoba. Be careful on the Nashville Road. It has become much more dangerous."

"The *Nashville* Road?" Zeb asked Dr. McAllister.

"Yes. When heading north on it toward Nashville, they call it the Nashville Road, not the Natchez Road."

The braves mounted and moved toward the gate. Hannah ran to open it. She stood in the street as they cantered toward the Nashville Road and Yowani.

◦∽◦

Even though he was hungry and the meal was wonderful, Zeb was eager to leave. But he hated to get up from the table before the others were finished. He looked up to find Hannah's mother smiling at him. "I know you're anxious to go, Zeb. Why don't you and Hannah get your horses tacked up and go over to Culpepper's farm to get Suba? Tack up that old bay for me, too. I just can't let Hannah out of my sight."

A short time later, Zeb, Hannah, and her mother passed through the outskirts of town and then turned the horses off the main road onto a narrow trail between two fenced fields. A number of horses grazed on the far side of one of the fields.

Hannah put two fingers in her mouth and whistled. A tall black mare lifted her head, her ears flicked forward. When Hannah whistled again, the mare broke away from the herd and galloped toward her. The other horses thundered toward the fence behind the mare.

The black horse put her head over the split-rail fence, her soft muzzle extended toward Hannah's outstretched hand. Hannah stroked Suba's face. "I'm home, Suba. I'm home," she murmured.

Suba turned her head and looked at Harlequin, the horse Hannah was riding. She stretched her neck, her nose close to his head. Suddenly, she squealed and leaped sideways, skittering along the fence.

A man on a large chestnut horse galloped toward them. "Private property!" he shouted. "Get away from those horses!"

The man pulled the horse in, clouds of dust settling around him. He was holding the reins in one hand, his other hand resting on a rifle in a saddle holster. He sat back as he recognized Hannah's mother. "Mrs. McAllister," he said. "What are *you* doing here? Is something wrong?" He lifted his chin toward Hannah and Zeb. "Who are these two boys?"

"Mr. Culpepper!" Hannah cried. "It's me! Hannah! I'm home! I've come to get Suba."

The man moved his horse so he was face-to-face with Hannah. He stared at her face and her short cropped hair and then at the Choctaw deerskin pants she was wearing. "Hannah! My dear child. I would never have recognized you. You're home! You're back! How wonderful! We all thought we would never see you again. Where have you been? What happened?"

Hannah's mother walked her horse closer to his. "We just thank God she is back with us."

Hannah reached out and put her hand on his arm. "I have to tell you all about it later, Mr. Culpepper." She raised her chin in Zeb's direction. "We need to take Suba back to the house so Zeb can ride her into Natchez."

Hannah turned Harlequin and moved back toward the gate. Zeb and Culpepper turned with her, riding three abreast. Hannah's mother followed behind.

"There's no way I can let you take Suba," Culpepper said. "She's much too spirited. She's been ridden every day, but not many could ride her on an open road, Hannah. She needs to be worked hard for a while in a corral."

"Thank you, Mr. Culpepper. We'll lead her home and then we'll see," Hannah replied. "If she's too hard to handle, we'll bring her back."

Suba, in the meantime, had galloped away, leading the other horses back to the far side of the field. When Hannah reached the gate, she vaulted off Harlequin, opened the gate, and stepped inside, holding Suba's bridle in her hand. She put her fingers in her mouth again, but even before she could whistle, Suba trotted, tail raised high, back to her. As Hannah approached her, Suba stretched her neck toward Hannah and then backed away.

Hannah turned from Suba and began to walk slowly toward the gate. Suba stepped forward quickly and put her head over Hannah's shoulder. Hannah reached up and stroked the horse's muzzle, slipping the reins over her head and the bit into her mouth. "You always fall for that, don't you, girl?"

She had used a curb bit with a short shank. Hannah looked up at Zeb. "I know how you feel about curb bits, Zeb, but no one would be able to manage Suba without it."

"We use curb bits with all the horses we train for the army," Zeb replied. "The sergeant was usin' a curb bit with an extra long shank and a roller. It's very painful, and can break a horse's jaw. That's why I didn't like it."

Culpepper looked closely at Zeb as if he had just noticed something about the young man.

Hannah led the horse out of the pasture and closed the gate behind her. She remounted Harlequin and then led Suba down the dirt road toward the McAllister house.

Mr. Culpepper rode with them next to Hannah's mother. He tipped his hat toward Mrs. McAllister. "Martha, I am glad Hannah's home safe and sound."

"Thank you," she said.

As he turned the horse back toward his farm he said, "Welcome home, Hannah. Mary Katherine will be relieved and happy to know you're home."

He looked at Zeb and appeared to be about to say something, but then tipped his hat again and cantered back the way he had come.

As they neared Hannah's house, Zeb could see Hannah's father standing on the front porch, waiting for them. Sarah was standing by the gate. Hannah and Zeb put Christmas, Harlequin, and Mrs. McAllister's horse back into the barn.

Zeb led Suba around the backyard, talking to her quietly. He stroked her long neck. "What a beautiful animal you are. We're gonna get along just fine," he whispered to her. The horse pulled back and then danced forward. "You're lettin' me know you're ready to run, aren't you? Calm down, atta girl, calm down."

A fine, misty rain was beginning to fall. Zeb handed Suba's reins to Hannah and jogged into the barn where he had left his tack. He returned with his bed roll and saddlebags and the piece of worn canvas that served as half of a small tent. "If it starts to rain hard," he said, "I can use this as a poncho."

"This rain won't last," Dr. McAllister said. "We get little sun showers almost every day at this time of year."

Suba lifted her head. Someone was coming down the road at an easy canter. "It's Katie!" Hannah shouted, and ran to open the gate.

A girl mounted on a dappled gray Arabian slowed the horse and then trotted her through the open gate and into the yard. The girl sat tall and completely at ease. She looked around the yard, her eyes passing over Hannah and then turning sharply back. "Hannah?" she said. "Is that you?"

Hannah smiled up at her.

The girl vaulted off the horse and ran to Hannah. "Oh, Hannah, Hannah, Father said I wouldn't recognize you. We all thought you were dead!"

Hannah moved quietly to where Zeb was standing with Suba. She took Suba's reins from him. "Katie, I want you to meet the person who brought me home, Zebulon D'Evereux from Franklin, Tennessee. Zeb, this is Mary Katherine Culpepper, my best friend."

The girl pulled off her hat, revealing hair the coppery color of the lamp Zeb's mama kept polished at home. Her hair was pulled back in a pony tail. Freckles spread across her cheeks and her nose.

Zeb nodded to her, and the girl smiled at him. "Father told me about you," she said. "He's coming here this afternoon to talk with you."

"I'm sorry," said Zeb, talking Suba's reins from Hannah. "I hafta get into Natchez as soon as possible. Maybe I'll see him when I get back."

Zeb saddled Suba and adjusted the stirrups to fit his long legs. He swung up on her and walked the horse around the yard, to the barn and back. Suba seemed calm and manageable, but Hannah grinned. "She's just waiting for you to get out on the road."

As he turned Suba toward the gate, Zeb could feel the horse's muscles tightening. She was ready to run.

CHAPTER THREE

The Search Begins

October 13, 1811

Zeb nodded at Hannah and headed toward Natchez. *Seems strange to be going someplace without Hannah,* he thought.

Suba wanted to run, and Zeb let her canter for short distances, but most of the time he kept her at a steady trot.

The sandy road into Natchez was wide and flat with no deep carriage ruts. The soil was slightly damp, and he could see the hoofprints of horses that had passed that way before him. The trees cast early afternoon shadows, and open fields of cotton stretched as far as he could see on both sides of the road.

Zeb paid the toll and crossed Catherine Creek. Suba started a little at the loud thumps of her hooves against the heavy wooden bridge timbers. Zeb pulled her in. "It's all right, Suba. Nothin' to worry about. Calm down. Atta girl."

Gradually the cotton fields gave way to a number of small houses clustered under the shade of ancient live oak trees. Not a weed or a blade of grass grew in the clean-swept yards.

Just ahead of him, Zeb could see a row of large houses on each side of the street. Many of the houses were made of squared-off, flatboat logs, weathered dark brown. Some of the newer-looking houses were built of milled lumber, painted white. Trees bordered the wide road. He was in Natchez, the place his grampa called "the cultural center of the South." *It probably is, at least for the part of the South that Grampa knows,* Zeb thought.

At the first cross street, Zeb saw a sign nailed to a tree with an arrow pointing left. Suba didn't want to stop. He had to keep turning her so he could read the sign.

ABSOLUTE AUCTION

h o r s e s

EVERY TYPE AND BREED

A FEW SELECT **RACEHORSES**

OCTOBER 12, 1811

TEXADA TAVERN, WASHINGTON AND WALL

SUNRISE TO DARK

There was no place he would be more likely to find his grampa than at a horse auction. Instead of going directly to King's Tavern, he turned Suba to the left and trotted up Pine Street. Then, following more arrows, he turned to the right on Washington Street, heading toward the river.

When Zeb got to Washington and Wall Streets, Texada Tavern was everything he had hoped it would be. It was the largest brick building he had ever seen. He was disappointed, though, not to find crowds of people milling around as they always do at a horse auction.

There was plenty of evidence on the dirt road that many horses had been there. *Could they have sold them all already?*

Zeb tied Suba to a rail and hurried into Texada Tavern. It took a few moments for his eyes to adjust to the darkness inside. The barroom, off to one side, was already crowded, but it wasn't boisterous like some of the stands on the Natchez Road. Men sat at tables, drinking and talking quietly. Others stood at a bar, drinking.

Behind the dark wooden bar, a man in a white shirt with arm garters holding his sleeves back sloshed two glasses at a time back and forth in a tub of soapy water.

Zeb stepped up to the bar. The bartender wiped the damp wood in front of Zeb with a wet cloth. "What can I get ya?"

"Don't want anything to drink. Want to find out about the horse auction."

"Horse auction?" the man said in a loud voice. He chuckled. "You're late, boy. That was yesterday. You buyin' or sellin'?"

Zeb sagged against the bar. *I'm a day late. I must've figured September for thirty-one days instead of thirty. Grampa could've come and gone. Now what?*

"I'm lookin' for someone. Someone I'm sure would've been at the auction. Did you see a—"

"Look," the bartender said, picking up a wet glass and drying it with a towel, "I didn't go to the auction. Never do. If he came in here, I might've seen him. But I doubt I'd remember."

Grampa wouldn't have come in here for a drink, Zeb thought.

Zeb was about to turn away when the bartender said, "You're in luck, boy. See that man just came in? Over there with the big leather hat? That's Dancey Moore. He buys and sells a lot of horses. If anyone'd know who was here, he would."

The bartender leaned over, lowering his voice to a whisper. "Just between you and me, boy, don't do no buyin' or sellin' with him 'less you got money to lose. He loves to take advantage of you Kaintucks."

Zeb looked down at his clothes. He wore a shirt and pants he had found in the throwaway box at Yowani, clean but ragged. He had no hat, and his borrowed boots were old and worn. *I look like a Kaintuck for sure.*

CHAPTER FOUR

Dancey Moore

October 13, 1811

Zeb stayed close to the dark walls as he moved over toward the man with the big leather hat. The man was now seated at a table, drinking and talking with someone who appeared to be a horse wrangler.

The man with the big leather hat wiped the dust off the table in front of him and turned to the wrangler. "You get everything taken care of?"

The wrangler leaned back in his chair. "Yeah. Drove those horses you bought over to the farm. You did pretty good this time without that old man biddin' against you."

"No problems?"

He shook his head. "Naw, just that family goin' west. Still want their money back. Said that horse you sold 'em is too sick to pull a wagon."

"Man don't know a sick horse from a healthy one shouldn't buy at a horse auction."

"Says he's gonna talk to the police constable."

"Won't do him no good. Absolute auction. Buyer beware!"

The horse wrangler didn't look convinced. "You might wanna do somethin', keep the constable from comin' around.

They're livin' in the wagon right now. They're outta money. Said if they hafta sell the wagon for enough money to eat, they'll dig one of them caves in the sand bluff to live in."

"Ha! That'll take care of the problem. The only people who live in 'em caves got nothin' to lose. They're just a bunch of criminals, runaway slaves, renegade Indians."

"I know, but—"

"Anytime a heavy wagon gets close to the edge of the bluff, some of those caves collapse. The police constable down in Natchez Under-The-Hill don't even bother goin' up there anymore. Those people move into a cave and we won't hear from 'em again."

Zeb knew that his grampa wouldn't have anything to do with men like these. Still, they might've seen him at the auction. He waited for a pause in their conversation. When another wrangler walked over, beat the dust out of his pants, and sat down with the two men, Zeb stepped forward. "Excuse me, sir? I wonder if I could talk with you for—"

The man waved him away. "Don't need no horse wranglers. Got all I need. Never hire Kaintucks if I can help it. Bone lazy and useless."

Zeb's clenched his teeth. He had made fun of the way Kaintucks talk all of his life. But these people in Natchez thought he was one. He made himself relax. "I'm not lookin' for a job, sir. I'm tryin' to find my grampa. Thought you might've seen him yesterday during the horse auction."

One of the men sitting at the table poked the other. "Maybe he's lookin' fer that crazy old coot, chased Willie Jones up the street with a bullwhip." They both laughed. They looked over at the man with the hat. "We didn't tell you 'bout that. Would've died laughin'."

Zeb could hardly breathe. *An old man with a bullwhip? It sounded like Grampa.* He knew that he had to be careful. Those men probably wouldn't tell him a thing if they thought it would help him. He tried not to show how interested he was. "Old man chased Willie Jones with a whip?" he asked.

"Yeah," one of them replied. "It was down on the docks. Willie bought him a horse and tried to load it onto a flatboat. You know how those ramps to the boats are pretty steep and slippery? That horse just wouldn't go—"

The other one interrupted. "Willie started pullin' on that horse and whippin' him with a long horse whip. The horse was screamin' and dancin' around, but he wouldn't go down the ramp."

"Yeah, and then this old coot, must be a hundred years old, bald as a cannon ball—"

The other one interrupted again. "He ain't bald. Got one a' them prison haircuts, shaved right down smooth. But you can see the white fuzz. It's growin' back."

"Anyway," continued the first storyteller, "he climbed down off a big Conestoga-type cotton wagon and took the whip away from Willie, real gentle like. He had his left hand in his shirt like his arm was hurtin'. Anyway, he put Willie's whip down on the ground and then he led the horse, nice as you please, down the ramp, talkin' to it the way the Choctaw do. Everybody cheered."

"Then the old coot came up the ramp. Willie had his hand in his pocket ready to give him a coin. The old coot pulled out his own whip and chased Willie down the street with it. He picked off Willie's hat without touchin' his head and then he got him a couple of good licks with it, too. I saw the dust fly outta his britches. Ever'body cheered and laughed. Willie ain't got too many friends."

Zeb closed his eyes. *Thank you, Lord,* he prayed.

The men at the table were silent for a moment. One of them looked up at Zeb. "That crazy old man your grampa? Been in prison, has he? No wonder yer lookin' fer him." He poked the other man in the ribs. "Hope ya find him 'fore Willie Jones does. That man's mean as a snake. Got a little Monongahela in him."

Zeb wasn't sure how much he should tell these men. The man with the big leather hat finally seemed to take some notice of Zeb. "What's your name, boy?"

"Zebulon D'Evereux, sir."

"And your grampa's name?"

"His name is Daniel Ryan, sir. Maybe you know him. He—"

One of the wranglers said, "Why, that's the man that—"

The man with the leather hat growled between his teeth. "Shut up! Keep yer stupid mouth shut!"

He turned to Zeb. "My name is Dancey Moore. I know Dan Ryan well. We're what you might call friendly competitors. We often bid on the same horses." One of the men smirked and Moore glared at him.

Mr. Moore snapped his fingers as if he had just remembered something. "I believe," he said, "that your grandfather will be down at the docks tomorrow to see about some horses. Get down there early. You'll want to stay here at the Texada tonight. It's where he usually stays now."

The man appeared calm and friendly, but Zeb noticed a little muscle twitch in his jaw.

Zeb thanked the three men for their help, moving toward the wooden screen that separated the bar from the rest of the inn. He didn't want them to see how excited he was. *Grampa alive!*

He stepped behind the screen and paused, listening to them arguing among themselves. "'Friendly competitors'? You'd swap yer squaw fer some a' the horses he's bought."

"Didn't that fellah McPhee tell you that Cracker Ryan was dead? Sold you his horse and saddle, didn't he? If he's still alive, you got problems. You know what he's like."

"How do you know he's gonna be down at the docks? No horses comin' tomorrow, just the cotton buyer."

"Shut up you two! I'm thinkin'."

Zeb turned away from the screen. *It has to be Grampa,* he thought. *But I wonder why he shaved his head? What was he doing on a cotton wagon?*

He approached a man sitting behind a big desk. "You the innkeeper?"

The man looked up from the papers on his desk and nodded.

"You ever have a man stay in the tavern name of Daniel Ryan? Big man with a lot of white hair, or with all his hair shaved off?"

The man shook his head. "You talkin' about Cracker Ryan? He ain't here. Never stays here. He always stays at King's Tavern. Ain't seen him for more than a month."

Zeb could still hear Dancey Moore and the other two men arguing in the barroom. He wondered why Dancey Moore tried to get him to stay at the Texada.

He stepped back out onto the front porch, planning to ride Suba over to King's Tavern, but several men stood around the horse, checking her legs and looking in her mouth. Zeb unhitched her, swung the reins over her head, and climbed up on the horse. One of the men held on to the bridle. "You plannin' to race this horse?" he asked.

"Naw," Zeb said, slack-jawed. "She ain't never done no

racin'. Doubt she could do more'n come in last. Y'all got racin' here in Natchez?"

The man holding on to the bridle squinted up at Zeb. "You ain't as backwoods as you sound. Ain't no Kaintuck be ridin' a horse like this one. Besides, that's a racin' saddle yer usin'."

He turned to the others, letting go of the bridle. "Bet we'll see this horse tonight."

Zeb, remembering the map Dr. McAllister had drawn for him, rode back up Washington Street, the way he'd come in to the Texada, and across to Jefferson, headed for King's Tavern.

He looked up. The tavern was just ahead. The dark, weathered wood gave the tavern a warm, welcoming look. He had heard so much about this place from his grampa that he felt almost as if he were home.

With the bedroll over his shoulder and the small saddlebag in his hand, Zeb stood in the entrance to King's Tavern. It was as dark inside as the Texada Tavern. A man looked up from a ledger and smiled. "You're in luck, boy. Every room but one is full. Cotton harvest. Two dollars for a bed. An extra dollar to board a horse."

Zeb walked carefully over to the table, trying to keep from marking the shiny waxed floor. "Thank you, sir," he said. "I'll be wantin' to stay tonight, at least. Longer, if I can make a little money. I'm lookin' for my grampa, name of Daniel Ryan. I know he stays here with you when he's in Natchez."

"You Dan Ryan's grandson? Guess I shoulda known it with that head of hair of yours."

He stood up and offered Zeb his hand. He was a stocky man with dark red hair turning gray. He wore a waistcoat over a ruffled white shirt. "I'm Henry King," he said. "Known your grandfather for years. I haven't seen him in quite a while, though. Been more than two months."

The man turned the guest register around and said, "Sign or make a mark. Here's a key to the room. Pick out the bed you want. But don't leave anything valuable up there. The other beds in that room will be taken before dark."

Zeb dropped the bedroll to the floor and picked up the quill. "Does the post rider still stop here?" he asked.

Mr. King nodded. "He should be here in the next couple of days."

"I wanna send a letter home."

Mr. King pointed to a wooden box with a slot on top. "Just put it in there when you have it ready. You got a horse?"

"Yes, sir."

"Then you'll need this." He handed Zeb a yellow card. "The stables are guarded. Show that to one of the men when you stable your horse and when you come to get it. Don't lose it!"

Zeb put the card in his shirt pocket.

Mr. King paused a moment. "You've never been here before?"

Zeb shook his head.

"Listen, son, Cracker Ryan and I are old friends. I want you to be very, very careful if you go down to Natchez Under-the-Hill."

Zeb nodded doubtfully. "I know. I can take care of myself."

Mr. King sighed. "You heard about the riverside taverns? No? A lot of their second stories hang out over the river. Men try to lure you in there, rob you, and then pull a trapdoor so you fall into the river. And don't hang about by the docks, because the press gangs might get you...." He shook his head. "Just watch yourself."

Zeb climbed the long flight of stairs to the second floor and then walked quietly down a narrow hallway to his room, glad this tavern was up in Natchez and not in Natchez Under-the-Hill. He would have to be careful.

I wish Hannah could see this place. King's Tavern is so different from the stands on the Natchez Road! This will be the first time I've slept in a bed since I left Franklin.

A light breeze through the open windows moved the curtains, throwing shadows on the wall. The beds were just like the ones they had at home. Ropes were tied from head to foot and from side to side about six inches apart, making a net to support the straw mattress rolled up at the head. It was tempting to unroll a mattress and try out one of the beds, but he wanted to see the Mississippi River before dark.

Zeb now had only two silver dollars.

CHAPTER FIVE

Isuba Lusa

October 13, 1811

It was late afternoon when Zeb mounted Suba. He could feel her gather herself, coiling tighter, ready to spring. Zeb pulled her up. She cantered in place, dancing sideways to the slightest pressure of either of his legs. "Easy girl! Easy!" he soothed her. "You'll have plenty of chances to run."

Nothing could calm her, so he let her trot briskly all the way to the river. When they got to the top of the bluff, high above the river, she was wet with sweat and so was Zeb, but she was now willing to walk. "I sure hope you didn't wear yourself out, Suba. You're gonna need all you've got for what I have in mind."

The Mississippi River was much wider than he had expected. Even though he was seated on Suba at the top of the bluff, Zeb could barely make out the other side.

A cluster of people stood quietly at the edge of the bluff, peering at the western sky.

"C'mon, Suba, let's see what they're lookin' at."

At the horizon, Zeb could see what looked like a shooting star, but much larger. It was like a ball of fire with two tails glowing behind it, and it didn't seem to be moving.

Zeb gulped. "Is that the comet?" he whispered to the people near him.

A man looked up at him and then back across the river. "Yep. Been up there, off and on, for a long time. You haven't seen it before this?"

"Nope. We live in a valley, and I've been travelin' down the Natchez Road for the last month or so. There's no place on the highway where you can see the horizon. But my friend Nashoba thinks it's a bad omen. He says somethin' terrible's gonna happen."

A woman nearby nodded her head in agreement. "I've heard talk of that, too." She shivered.

After a while, Zeb drifted away from the river's edge.

Lights began to come on in the buildings along the river-front a hundred feet or more below him. Even at this hour, flat-boats moved from upriver into the docks. *So that's the place they call Natchez Under-The-Hill.*

Zeb headed south until he found Silver Street, a steep cobblestone road that led to the docks. Suba slipped on the wet cobblestones. Zeb halted her and dismounted, leading the horse slowly down the hill.

Someone shouted, "Hey! You there! I'm talkin' to you, boy!"

Zeb recognized the four men who had been so interested in Suba up at the Texada Inn. They were just coming out of a tavern. One of the men walked over and patted Suba's wet neck. "Been runnin', has she? Thought you said you ain't gonna race this horse."

"Hadn't planned to. Changed my mind. I need the money."

"She fast?"

"She's fast all right, but—"

"What are you hidin', boy? You playin' some kinda game?"

Zeb shook his head. "No, sir," he said. "I just don't know if she's got the stamina. Never raced in competition. She's fast, though, and wants to run. Fought me all the way down here."

The man squinted at Zeb, his eyes locking on to Zeb's the way Zeb's grampa's eyes would look at a horse trader he didn't know. "You tellin' me the truth, boy? This horse never raced before?"

"That's right."

"You signed up yet?"

"No," Zeb replied. "I don't know where the track is."

"Listen, boy," he said. "You wait until the last minute to sign up. We may be able to give a little surprise to some folks I know."

"Tell me what the track is like."

"This race isn't on the official track. That track's a straight quarter mile from bluff to river or river to bluff. This race is rough-and-ready. They rope off some of the dirt streets. You ride up a block, shorter than the ones you find in Natchez, across one, down a block, and across another one. You do that twice. The whole race is just under a mile. And one other thing. On the first lap it's a good idea to stay in the outside lane 'cause of the sharp turns."

"Who'll I be racin' against?"

"There'll be four or five nags ridden by the local boys. There'll be one or two fools from the plantations who think they have a chance, and there'll be a real racehorse from the racetrack up in Natchez, down here to scoop up all the money."

Suba lifted her head. "Hear that trumpet, boy?" the man said, pointing to an area downriver from Silver Street. "Race starts in ten minutes. You go on over and enter your horse." He winked at the other men. "We'll be right behind you."

The organizer of the race sat on a bench on a wooden stand built high enough so that he was eye-to-eye with the jockeys. "That'll cost you two dollars," the organizer said to Zeb. "First place wins twenty-five dollars and second place wins five dollars." He handed Zeb two straight pins and a sheet of paper with the number eight on it. "That'll be your number, boy. Pin it to the front of your shirt."

He looked at Zeb without paying much attention to Suba. "You haven't raced here before, have you? Two laps around, a little less than a mile. This is the judges' stand." He motioned toward it. "And this line," he said, pointing to a white line chalked across the road, "is the start and finish line. If it's a close race, judges decide. When the gun goes off, just race your horse. Don't pay any attention to what anyone says or does. False start is another shot of the gun. Got that?"

Zeb nodded and rode away. He realized that the big money changed hands through the bets made by the spectators. *Too bad,* Zeb thought, *that I don't have a little more money with me and I don't have Christmas to race.*

He circled Suba behind the start line. Five other horses were already there. The boys who were riding them were cussing at each other and shoving, trying to get the position nearest the inside lane. Zeb moved Suba to the outside. He figured she was fast enough to move in once she got the lead. Two horses moved up from behind him, one on either side.

Someone from the judges' stand shouted, "Move back, you boys, or you'll be disqualified! Back behind that white line! All right now…riders ready?"

The gun went off. In a single movement, all the riders kicked their mounts, and the horses burst into a gallop. Zeb suddenly found himself sandwiched between two horses. He felt a yank on his belt. Someone was trying to pull him off! He was out of the saddle! One more pull and he would be on the ground.

He lashed out with his arm and felt the hand let go of his belt. Suba was running at a full gallop. Zeb grabbed hold of the pommel, pulling himself back onto the saddle. He couldn't get his feet back into the stirrups, so he rode Suba without them, his legs clamped around her body and the stirrups banging against his ankles.

A horse Zeb hadn't seen before was coming up behind him.

A racing whip slashed across his mouth. He licked his lip and tasted blood. The two horses had him sandwiched again. One of the boys slammed his fist against Zeb's ribs. Zeb held on.

Luckily, Suba took to racing the way Christmas did. She broke away from the two horses and was soon just behind the leader. When Zeb squeezed his legs, Suba edged slightly ahead of the leading horse. As they neared the end of the first lap, it seemed to be a race just between Suba and the leader. The others were lengths behind.

Suba inched past the other horse. As soon as there was room, Zeb moved her toward the inside, keeping the other horse from passing. When Zeb passed the judges' stand, he was in the lead for the second lap.

He grabbed a fistful of mane to steady himself and peered under his outstretched arm to see how close the other horses were. A horse he hadn't seen before was coming up behind him. *Must be the racehorse they told me about.*

The racehorse was gaining on his right. Zeb squeezed his legs, leaned forward, and shouted against the wind and fine dust biting into his face. "Come on, girl! You can do it. Don't let that pretty boy beat you."

Suba sensed the urgency. She lengthened her stride and moved faster than Zeb had known even Christmas to run. They passed the marker in front of the judges' stand a length in front of the racehorse. Zeb let her take another turn of the track to slow down. Then he sat back, slipping his feet into the stirrups, his body relaxed. He smiled and clapped the horse's neck. He wished Hannah had been here with him, so she could have seen her horse win. Suba didn't even seem to be very tired.

He heard the announcement from the judge's stand. "The winner is number eight. Second place goes to number six."

At first it was strangely quiet. Then, as he rode past a cluster of men standing near the finish line, a man called out to him. "Better not come back here, boy."

The four men from outside the Texada Inn were laughing and pounding each other on the back. He grinned at them as he rode by, wincing a bit at the pain in his swollen lip.

When Zeb approached the judges' stand, the race organizer reached out and grabbed hold of Zeb's shirt, pulling Zeb toward him. Zeb halted Suba to keep from being yanked out of the saddle, but Suba sidled away from the man, not yet ready to stand still.

"I'll give you a thousand for that horse," the man said in a low voice. "No questions asked."

"Sorry, sir," Zeb said. "The horse is not for sale."

Dancey Moore was sitting just behind the organizer. "I'll give you a thousand," he said to Zeb, "and throw in a good saddle horse to boot." When Moore spoke, he looked away. Zeb had seen horse traders that wouldn't look you in the eye. Grampa didn't trust them.

Zeb shook his head. "The horse is not for sale at any price," he said.

Moore smiled at him. "Everything has its price, kid, as you'll find out sooner or later."

Moore seemed to be making an effort to be friendly. "By the way," he added, "there'll be bareback racing in about an hour. One turn around the track. Most of the same boys'll be ridin'. That race shows who the real riders are. You could make a lot of money. Bet your horse against my one thousand dollars. Course, if you can't ride bareback...."

A thousand dollars! Suba could beat any horse here. Zeb wondered why Moore was trying to goad him into racing bareback. He must know that Zeb would have no trouble. *A thousand dollars!*

He could feel his heart pounding in his ears. *A thousand dollars! With that much money, I could buy a small farm! Or five good saddle horses. I'd have enough to offer a reward to help find Grampa.*

He shook his head. The very thought reminded him of what his grampa often said whenever he found out that Zeb was racing Christmas. "One day," the old man would say, "you'll bet your horse, and you'll lose it."

No point in thinking about it. He couldn't bet Suba anyway. Wasn't his horse. Besides, with all that pushing and shoving, it might be hard to stay on riding bareback. And if he got hurt, who would find Grampa?

He looked once again at Moore. *Maybe that is what this is all about,* he thought. *Maybe Moore is trying to keep me from finding Grampa!*

Zeb shook his head. "Don't think I'll do it," he said. "Not much good at bareback ridin'. Besides, Suba needs to rest."

Dancey Moore glared at him. "Got a lot of your grampa in you, don't you? We'll see what good it'll do you."

Zeb shrugged. He pulled his wet shirt away from his chest and unpinned the paper, surprised that it was still in one piece. He wove the two pins back into the paper, handing it to the judge. The judge counted four golden half-eagles into his hand, holding on to the last five-dollar coin until he had Zeb's attention. "You change your mind," he said, "you can always find me up at the Natchez racetrack."

Zeb checked carefully to be sure that the coins were U.S. money, not Spanish or French. He lifted his head. "I'm not gonna change my mind," he said.

Zeb decided to leave the horse at King's Tavern for the night. He didn't like all the interest in Suba. *If they're willing to pay a thousand dollars for the horse, what else would they be willing to do?* He rode Suba back through the dock area and up Silver Street to Natchez.

He headed north along the river bluff until he saw the big white house on the hill. Turning right on Jefferson, he suddenly stopped Suba and turned her back to a building on one of the corners. The sign on the window said *Natchez Weekly Chronicle.* Zeb noted where he was and then let Suba continue on to King's Tavern.

At the stable, Zeb pulled the sweat-stained yellow card out of his shirt pocket and handed it to one of the stablemen. "I'd appreciate it," he said, "if you'd water her and give her some feed in about an hour. She's been runnin' hard."

The man looked up at him, holding on to the bridle. "She's a lot calmer than when ya left here. Expected to see ya walkin' back on yer own two feet."

Zeb slipped off Suba. When he started to take off her saddle, the stableman stopped him. "We'll do all that." He ran his hand down Suba's long wet neck. "She's a beauty, ain't she? We'll be sure to wash 'er down and give 'er a good brushin'."

Zeb marveled at life in Natchez. He had never had anyone brush and comb his horse for him. He wasn't sure he liked it.

He went on foot back to the river and down the cobble-stone road to Natchez Under-the-Hill to spend the evening. He had heard a lot about this place. Letters published in his uncle's newspaper in Franklin made it sound like the worst place in the Mississippi territory, maybe the worst place in the whole United States. One person, returning to Franklin, had written that there was "Natchez Proper" and "Natchez Improper." And Mr. King had just warned him about the dangers that afternoon.

Zeb, of course, was intrigued.

CHAPTER SIX

Natchez Under-the-Hill

October 14, 1811

arly the next morning, Zeb rode to the top of Silver Street and looked down at the river and the taverns along its edge. Dancey Moore had said his grampa would be at the docks in Natchez Under-The-Hill very early. Zeb didn't really believe him, but he couldn't take a chance of missing his grampa.

In the early light, the river port had a sad, tattered, morning-after look. The mist from the big river flowed up the side streets like a dirty gray curtain hastily pulled against the rising sun. Zeb shivered in the cold, wet air.

It had been so appealing last night: the aroma of fried fish and his first taste of hot, spicy jambalaya; riverboat music on homemade fiddles; and men's raucous, drunken singing.

Now, pigs pushed their urgent noses through the garbage pile just outside a kitchen door, the acrid odor of pig excrement mixing with the stench of rotting fish heads and crawfish shells. A woman leaned over a balcony on the third floor, emptying a chamber pot onto the alley below.

Zeb dismounted and led Suba down the slippery cobblestone street. He ran his hand down her smooth neck, the long muscles rippling under his hand as she turned her head toward him. He could feel her soft nostrils and her warm breath against his cheek.

Except for the woman on the balcony, not a soul seemed to be awake. Zeb looked back over his shoulder, sensing that someone was watching him. There was no one in sight.

He was beginning to wonder if he should have come down here to the docks alone. The only sound he could hear was the clopping of Suba's hooves on the cobblestones. He listened carefully, as alert as he had been on the Natchez Road, walking with one hand on the pistol stuck in his belt.

A low groan came from the alley to his left. He stopped and looked. Someone was lying in the alley. *Probably just a drunk sleeping it off,* he thought. When he stepped closer, he gasped. Even though the man was lying on his back, Zeb could see that he was huge. Larger even than the sergeant. He had a mass of honey-colored hair and a shaggy mustache of the same color that almost covered his mouth. He was holding his chest and moaning.

The man opened his eyes and stared at Zeb for a moment. "Hey there, boy," he groaned. "Give us a hand. Jumped by six. Left me for dead." He lifted his head. "Give us a hand, boy."

Zeb looked down at the man, wondering if it wouldn't be wise just to ignore him and move on. Maybe he wasn't hurt at all. Maybe he was part of one of Dancey Moore's games.

The man looked up at him again. "Come on there, boy! Give us a hand."

Zeb stepped closer with one hand on his pistol. He could see the dried blood on the man's face and on the backs of his hands. There was no doubt he'd been in a fight.

Zeb tied Suba to a rail and pushed the pistol back in his belt. He reached down with both hands to the man's out-stretched arm. At first, it seemed impossible to budge him.

Finally, the man got up on his knees and then struggled to his feet, groaning and holding on to his side.

He towered over Zeb. His clothes were damp with whiskey and blood. He looked down at Zeb and his pistol. "You plannin' to shoot me?"

"I ain't made up my mind yet. Everybody says you can't be too careful down here."

Zeb guided him to the horse. "Do you think you can mount?"

The man shook his head. "No," he said, "don't think so. Think I got a broken rib or two. But I kin hold on to the horse with one hand, if you'll hold me up with the other."

Zeb positioned himself on the other side of the big man and they made their way through the alley behind the taverns toward a small tavern at the river's edge. The front of the tavern faced the water. A row of molasses barrels stood at the back, near a pile of staves and barrel hoops ready to be assembled.

The big man leaned over and opened his mouth to whisper to Zeb. The sour, sick smell of his breath made Zeb turn his head away. "You get me in there," the big man said, "with nobody bein' the wiser, and I'll make it worth yer while."

They got to the back of the tavern without seeing anyone. Zeb tied Suba to a post. He looked around. "Where's your horse?" he whispered.

The big man shook his head. "Don't you know nothin', boy?" he said in a loud whisper. "I don't got no horse. Don't need one. I work the flatboats. I'm cock o' the walk and don't you ferget it! Ain't nobody can whup me in a fair fight."

The man leaned against the doorway and moaned. "Come on, boy," he whispered. "I ain't got all day."

Zeb helped the man through the back door of the tavern and up the stairs. When they reached the landing, the man staggered against the wall, knocking a picture to the floor. "Can't you be more quiet, boy?" he hissed.

He put his hand inside his shirt. Zeb stepped back, his hand on his pistol. He knew that the Kaintucks on the Natchez Road carried their knives or their guns inside their shirts. The man grinned at him and pulled out a big brass key. "You're smart to be careful, boy. You'll live longer." He handed the key to Zeb. "That door over there, lad." He gestured wildly. He could have meant any one of three rooms. "And do be quiet about it," he said.

When Zeb headed for the door that led to the front room, the one that hung over the river, the big man grabbed Zeb by the back of his shirt. "Not that one, you fool! You go in that one, yer never seen again!"

Zeb opened the next door and led the man into the room. The man staggered over to the bed, turned around, and fell on it. He was lying on his back, his arm still clutched to his chest, his face in a grimace. Suddenly, his arm relaxed and fell to his side. He seemed to be unconscious or already in a deep sleep. Zeb closed the door, locked it from the outside, and pushed the key under the door.

He took the back stairs to the alley where he had left Suba. A police constable was standing next to her. "This your horse?" the constable asked.

"No, sir," Zeb said, smiling. "Belongs to a friend. I have a letter of authorization right here with me—"

"What's your name, lad?"

"I'm Zebulon D'Evereux, sir, and this here is Suba."

The constable glared at him, and Zeb's smile faded. He could barely speak above a whisper. "What's the matter?"

The constable reached over and pulled the pistol from Zeb's belt. With the other hand he took out a sheet of paper.

The man staggered against the wall, knocking a picture to the floor.

"Zebulon D'Evereux, I arrest you on suspicion of kidnapping. Put your hands behind your back."

"Kidnapping!" he cried out. "Are you talkin' about Hannah? I didn't kidnap her! She came with me."

The constable nodded. "So you admit it. Turn around and put your arms behind you."

Zeb turned around. "I found her on the Natchez Road. She ran away from the Mason gang. She—"

"Be quiet!" The constable tied a leather thong around Zeb's wrists. "You'll have your chance in court." He pushed Zeb ahead of him.

"Wait!" Zeb shouted, pulling frantically at the leather thong on his wrists. He had heard terrible stories about the jail up in Nashville. This one couldn't be any better. "Please don't put me in jail. I haven't done anything wrong!"

The constable pulled the thong tighter. "That's for the magistrate to decide," he growled.

Zeb looked back at Suba. "But what will happen to the horse? You can't just leave that horse there. She belongs to Hannah...."

The constable shoved him forward. "You should have thought about that before you decided to kidnap a child for ransom."

As they turned the corner, Zeb pleaded with him again. "Just look in my shirt pocket," he shouted. "I have a letter authorizing me to ride Suba. It was signed by Hannah's father yesterday."

They looked up and found themselves face to face with the sergeant. "Well!" the sergeant said. "You've found the little varmint. You leave him here with me, Constable, and you'll have a confession within the hour."

Zeb tugged furiously at the thongs tied around his wrists. "You can't leave me with him! He wants to kill me."

The constable yanked on the thongs making them even tighter. "You be quiet! That's my last warning!" He turned to the sergeant. "There's no need for you to do anything. He already confessed."

Zeb yanked his hands down, trying to break the rawhide. "I didn't confess!" he shouted. "I told you that she came with me. I found her on the trail, she...."

The constable grabbed Zeb's chin and forced him to look at him. "I told you to be quiet. You'll have plenty of time to talk when you go before the magistrate."

"But the sergeant is—"

"I told you, not one more word!"

The sergeant walked along with them as they moved toward the end of the street. "Just turn him over to me and you won't even hafta worry about a trial," he said.

The constable stopped and looked at the sergeant. "Just what is your interest in all of this, Sergeant? You have been drummed out of the army. You have no official status here. If you are after a reward, I will testify that you and Dancey Moore are the ones who made the official complaint and showed us how to find him."

He looked at Zeb. "A tall, lanky boy, with a lot of shaggy hair, riding a black horse, due to come down here first thing this morning."

He turned back to the sergeant. "Now, please go about your business. I will take care of the prisoner."

The constable yanked Zeb around and pushed him through a doorway in a brick building that backed up against the sandy bluff. The constable looked at Zeb with disgust. "I've only got one cell left. It's for drunks and barroom brawlers. You'll be alone for now, but you'll probably have company tonight. It's too good for a kidnapper, but that's where you're going, my boy."

After untying the leather thong from around Zeb's wrists, the constable opened the heavy wooden door. Zeb tried to run past him but the man grabbed him around the neck and gave him a final hard shove into the room. He slammed the door.

Zeb tripped and slid across the slippery stone floor to a wall. He could not see a thing. There were no windows, nor light of any kind. He sat up and leaned against the wall, feeling the damp stones against his back. He put his hand on the floor. What made it so slippery? He sniffed his hand and gagged, wiping his hand over and over again on his pants.

He listened. He could hear scratching quite near him. He reached out his hand and ran it down the rough stones of the wall to the floor. His hand touched a furry body. He screamed, snatching his hand away. He stood up and stomped the floor around him. Rats! The place was full of rats!

Zeb moved carefully against the wall to see how large the cell was. Turning, he walked along the second wall, which was also stone, with the big wooden door in the middle.

The third wall was stone and mortar, but it was dripping wet. He paced along that wall. *Must be about twelve feet long.* When he touched the next wall, he was surprised. It was dirt! The room had been cut into the side of the bluff.

He had noticed that the bluff was that same strange, coarse, loamy sand that he and Hannah had seen the last several days on the Natchez Road. He recalled Dancey Moore's men saying that people dug caves in the sandy bluffs and lived in them. *Maybe I can dig my way out of this place.* He ran his hand along the wall. It was smooth. No gouged-out places. *The drunk prisoners are probably kept here until they sleep it off. No need to try to scratch their way out.*

He slid back down to the floor. *How could they think I'd kidnap Hannah? What am I gonna do? What will happen to Suba? If*

Grampa is alive, he doesn't know that McPhee's men were following us to Natchez. I've gotta find him before they do.

He stood up and walked from one side of the cell to the other, dragging one foot, trying to see if there was anything in the room he could use to dig out the wall.

The door latch creaked. Zeb was about to complain about the lack of minimal necessities when he heard the constable shout, "Sergeant! What are you doing there? You have no business in this jail. If I find you in here again, I'll throw you into a cell. Now, get out!"

"Just a matter of simple justice," the sergeant replied, moving away.

The constable opened the door, letting in a little light from the hallway. He handed Zeb a chamber pot. "You'll need this," he said. "I'll have something for you to eat in a little bit. I'm beginning to wonder about all of this. What is the sergeant's interest, anyway?"

Zeb was so grateful for the dim light from the open door, he hoped he could keep the constable talking.

"He's after revenge," Zeb said. "He blames me for what happened to his hand." Zeb thought that the constable looked a little less hostile than before. "Listen," Zeb said, "I am not a kidnapper." He reached into his shirt. "Take a look at the paper I have. It was written by Hannah's father yesterday."

The constable shook his head. "It wouldn't make any difference. It's not for me to decide. The sergeant has sworn that you are the kidnapper of Hannah McAllister. Dancey Moore told us how to find you. You'll have to go before the magistrate. He won't be here for a couple of days." He was about to close the door when he turned and said, "I'm sorry to tell you that when I went back to get the horse to stable it as evidence, it was gone." He closed the big door and left Zeb in the dark once more.

Zeb held the pot in his two hands. If he could have, he would have ripped it in half. He leaned back against the wall and slid once more to the floor. *Now what'll I do? The sergeant already has Suba, and even if I can dig out of here, it'll probably take hours. I'm sorry, Hannah. I never should've raced Suba. I never should've brought her down here.*

He put his hand on the damp, slippery floor and stood back up. *I've gotta try it.*

Zeb took the chamber pot and felt his way back to the sandy wall. *I'll have to hurry or it'll be too late.* After he had scraped through the hard-packed crust, he found the earth soft and easy to move. He dug with the pot until he had created a fairly large hole. He knew he couldn't continue straight back; at some point, he had to turn and dig around the stone wall. But maybe he would just emerge from the sandy bank into another cell. *Are there cells on either side of mine?*

He tried to remember the entrance to the building, the passageway to the cells, and the little turn to this cell. *The wall on the left side facing the door,* he remembered, *is open to the passageway. I ought to be able to dig around it.*

He moved along the dirt wall until he was standing next to the stone wall. Then he got down on his hands and knees and started to dig again, careful not to bang the pot against the wall. The moisture in the earth seemed to hold it together.

He dug as fast as he could, throwing the moist sand behind him into the dark cell. It worked all right until his head and shoulders were inside the tunnel. Then he had to scoop out the sand and crawl backward to empty the pot. That slowed him down, but he kept at it until his arms ached. He was just creeping back in the tunnel when he heard a soft *thunk* and felt the vise-like grip of heavy, wet sand on his lower back. The entrance to the tunnel had caved in!

His first instinct was to throw himself backward, but he couldn't move. He patted the roof of the tunnel with his hands. That part was still open.

Slowly...slowly, he told himself. *Any sudden movement can bring the whole tunnel down on top of me. Keep calm.* He breathed deeply but carefully, thankful that there was still some air in the tunnel. He pushed his hands against the tunnel floor, twisting his body from side to side. As he wriggled backward, he reached out for the chamber pot, dragging it with him.

The dirt held. The saddle of sand felt lighter and lighter. With one more twist, he wrenched his body out of the tunnel and fell back in his cell. He kept his head down, his eyes closed, carefully brushing the damp sand from his face. He turned over and sat on the damp cell floor, gasping for breath.

Now what?... Maybe I should just wait here in the cell for the magistrate. Constable said it might be a couple of days...but what about Grampa?

He clenched his jaw in frustration. *That must be what Dancey Moore wants, to keep me out of the way until the sergeant can steal Suba, and they can hide her somewhere...and maybe keep me from finding Grampa.*

Zeb began over again, digging out the tunnel entrance. He reached in and patted the walls and the roof of the tunnel. They seemed to be holding. He took a couple of big breaths and pushed himself back into the narrow hole. He had already reached the end of the wall before the cave-in. Now he would have to turn and go the other way.

He started the new tunnel, digging and crawling backward with each potful of soil. He dug as fast as he could, trying to keep from disturbing the fragile walls. His body was folded around the wall, his legs still in the first tunnel and his upper body in the tunnel on the other side.

45

He twisted back and forth until he was free.

Afraid to move, he stopped for a moment. *Oh, no!* Loose, dry sand was filling the place in front of him that he had just dug. He filled the pot and then squirmed to back around the corner. His shoulder touched the roof of the tunnel. It quivered and then sand began to pour on top of him. It was heavy on his hips and waist. He couldn't move backward at all.

He held the pot in front of his face with both hands, pushing forward, straining, trying to make some breathing room. It was completely dark. There was very little air left. He relaxed his arms for a moment and rested. Then he pushed as hard as he could with the pot. *The sand is holding! It isn't caving in!* He pushed again, digging with his toes, trying to move his body forward.

One more push.... There was dim light coming through the sand! He must be near the end. He wiggled his body from side to side, pushing with the pot until the wall in front of him gave way. He forced his head and shoulders into the empty corridor.

Zeb lay there breathing deeply, almost sobbing. He could feel the sand inside the tunnel tightening its grip on him from his waist down. He put the pot down quietly and then twisted until he was on his back. Digging with his heels against the tunnel floor, he twisted back and forth until he was free.

He wiped the sand off his face, trying to keep it from getting into his eyes. Then he staggered to his feet, gasping for breath. *No one in sight...no sound, either.* He crept down the hall, praying that the huge oak door would not be locked.

He turned the handle carefully and pushed on the door. It began to swing open, the old rusty hinges groaning with the effort. He opened the door just enough to edge through, closed it behind him, and then darted into the shade of the alley between the jail and the building next door.

CHAPTER SEVEN

Grampa

October 14, 1811

Zeb found himself in an alley with only one way out. He started to move in that direction but he stopped when he heard someone crying, someone who might see him and call the constable. He crept forward and peeked around the edge of the building.

It was Hannah! She was sitting on the front steps of the jail, her head on her knees, sobbing her heart out.

Zeb whispered loudly to her, "Hannah!"

She didn't hear him. He called her again. "Hannah!" and even louder, "*Hannah!*"

She turned her head and screamed, "Zeb! You're alive!" She jumped up and ran to him, throwing her arms around him. "C'mon!" she said frantically, grabbing his hand and pulling him toward the jail. "They're sure you're dead, or buried alive!" She tugged at his arm. "C'mon! Father and the constable are in there, still digging at the back wall of that cell. The sand keeps caving in on them. We've gotta let them know you're alive!"

Zeb pulled back and shook his head. "I'm sorry, Hannah. I can't. The sergeant stole Suba and I hafta go find her."

"Oh, Zeb!" Hannah cried. "How could you let him steal Suba from you?"

"He told the constable I was a kidnapper, so he could steal her when I was in jail. The constable went back to get her a few minutes after he arrested me, and she was already gone."

"What'll we do?"

"I'll find her, Hannah. They can't have gone far."

"What about your grampa?"

"I heard a horse wrangler talking yesterday about a man mistreating a horse, and a bald-headed man chasin' him down the street with a whip. It sounded just like something my grampa would do. I can't imagine him bald, but that's what I'm gonna look for. They said he comes down here to the cotton buyer drivin' a big freight wagon. So after I find Suba, I'll go to the cotton auction down at the docks."

He looked at the jail. "Hannah, I want you to give me time to get away, then go in and tell them I'm all right. Tell your father I've gone lookin' for Suba and then I'm gonna look for Grampa.... Go now."

Hannah turned and ran up the stairs to the jail-house door. She turned and called down to him, "I'll keep an eye out for a big wagon and a bald man." She opened the door and stepped inside.

Zeb moved as quickly as he could, staying in the shadow of the buildings. He ran across the street and through an alley to Water Street. He raced from one building to the next, checking the horses tied up in front.

Zeb ran through an alley to Levee Street, where the taverns were all built at the water's edge. Flatboats serving as docks floated in front of some of them.

He skidded to a halt. A row of molasses barrels and piles of staves and hoops! This was where the constable had arrested him and this was the little tavern where he had helped the man slip up to his room.

Zeb edged in between the barrels and tried to make his way, unseen, around to the front of the tavern. One of the two wranglers he had seen with Dancey Moore was sitting on the porch. Zeb gasped. Tethered to the rail in the alley next to him were two horses. One of them was a broad black gelding, with four white stockings and a white snip on his nose. There was no doubt about it. It was Andy, Grampa's horse.

He stood there a moment. *It's tempting to take Andy and come back to look for Suba, but then Suba might be gone forever. And if I do take Andy and they catch me, they might hang me for stealing him. I have no proof that Andy is Grampa's horse.* Zeb slipped behind the man and moved quietly through the front door.

As his eyes adjusted to the dark interior, he could see Dancey Moore and the sergeant at a table right next to the door. Mr. Moore was counting out money into the sergeant's left hand. The sergeant held his other hand behind his back.

He was being paid for Suba! Zeb was torn between his wanting to challenge the two men and knowing that he really didn't have a chance with them. He was about to back out of the room when the sergeant raised his eyes and saw him. The sergeant leaped to his feet and blocked the door. "Well, well, well," he chortled, "how Lady Luck can smile on me! I have the money for your horse, and now I've got you. Police constable let you go? Miss Hannah show up?"

Zeb tried to keep his eyes on the sergeant while he looked around the little tavern for another way out.

"You can forget about that," the sergeant growled. "There ain't no other way out of here. Just you and me now, boy, settling up accounts." He began to move closer to Zeb.

"You can't sell Suba!" Zeb shouted. "She's a registered horse that belongs to the McAllisters."

"And you got a paper to prove it. I know. I heard."

He grabbed Zeb around the neck and reached into Zeb's shirt pocket. "That's all we need to make it legal," he snarled. He tossed the paper on the table in front of Dancey Moore.

The sergeant shoved Zeb away from him but stayed between Zeb and the door. He moved toward Zeb, playing with him, keeping his right hand behind him. *What does he have?* Zeb wondered. *A pistol? A knife?*

Zeb looked from one side to the other. He could see nothing to use as a weapon. The sergeant grinned, swinging his left fist hard as if he were aiming at Zeb's face.

Zeb ducked back and felt a low blow to the ribs. The sergeant laughed. "You don't know nothin' about fightin', do you? This'll be your first and maybe your last lesson." He swung again with his left hand.

This time, Zeb stepped back and then kicked hard at the sergeant's knee. The sergeant howled. "I was just gonna mess up that face a bit," he shouted. "Teach you a lesson. But now, it's no holds barred!" He reached out with both arms. His right hand held no weapon. It couldn't. The hand was misshapen, and he was missing two fingers.

The sergeant glared at him. "That's right. You're responsible for that hand. I told you then that I'd make you pay."

"Sergeant!" A booming voice rang out from above them. The big man Zeb had helped earlier was standing on the inside stairs, looking down at them. He was wearing the same wrinkled, stained clothes he had on when Zeb found him. "You talkin' 'bout fightin' with the partner of Lonnie Champ?" he roared. "The roughest, meanest cock o' the walk on the Mississippi? Thought I already spanked ya oncet. Looks like it didn't take. You lookin' at an alligator, a water snake, a black bear! You'd best run while ya can!"

The sergeant backed away and then edged toward the door. He held his hands up. "He your partner, Mr. Champ? We didn't know that, sir…honest!"

The man on the stairs looked over at Zeb. He lifted his chin toward the door. "You best leave, boy, and now."

Zeb started to mention the papers and the horse. The man pointed outside. "Now!" he shouted.

Zeb moved behind the sergeant and slipped out the door. He wished he could go to the constable, but he knew it was no use. "I can't do a thing about it," the constable had said when Zeb showed him the letter. "We have to wait for the magistrate."

A groaning rumble came from the dock area downriver from where he was standing, and above the low rumble he heard the voices of men shouting. Freight wagons come to market!

He hurried down toward the docks, darting from one alley to the next, constantly watching for the constable. A long line of wagons snaked down Silver Street, the steep and slippery cobblestone road from Natchez proper.

At the docks, the wagons were jammed together. He could see a child darting from one wagon to the next. *That kid's gonna get himself killed,* he thought. He gasped. It was Hannah!

She waved when she saw him, then crossed in front of two nervous horses and ran to his side, breathing hard. "Zeb," she said, "I found the bald man."

"You found him?"

"Ran up to the top of Silver Street. Bald man's ridin' in a big Conestoga wagon, just like the one Mr. Culpepper has. Six bales of cotton. Four big gray horses."

"Where is it?"

"Just come down Silver Street. Should be about halfway to the docks by now."

Zeb grabbed her arm. "Let's go."

"It may not be him, Zeb," she cautioned, running alongside him. "I got as close as I could and I yelled up to him, 'Mr. Ryan?' He looked down at me, shook his head, and kept on going."

When they reached the cotton docks, dozens of wagons were already there. Most of the wagons had a black driver and a white farmer sitting on the wagon seat.

One of the wagons was the largest he had ever seen, slanted up on the front and the back like a boat. It was carrying six bales of cotton instead of the usual four. Four huge draft horses pulled the wagon as easily as if it were empty.

Driving the wagon was a black man and at his right side a bald old white man. *That can't be grampa,* he told himself. *Grampa never lets anybody else drive a team of four, and he'd never wear overalls.*

Zeb was about to move away from the wagon when he spotted the coiled whip on the man's belt. *Maybe that is Grampa, or somebody who has his whip.*

Zeb and Hannah ran across the street toward the huge wagon, trying to fight their way between the wagons and around the horses. The wagons were jammed together, each of the drivers trying to be the first in line. Zeb got through and climbed up on the back of the wagon. He yelled down to Hannah, "Wait until I make sure who it is."

He pulled himself over the bales, yelling, trying to be heard over the shouts and curses of the wagon drivers. He kept looking at that bald head. The man's head was pink with sunburn, but his neck was dark brown and leathery. *Why isn't he wearing a hat?*

He climbed over the last bale, landing on the seat between the two men. The black man shouted, "What the!…" then swung his right arm, knocking Zeb back against the cotton

*Driving the wagon was a black man and at his side a
bald old white man.*

bales. The old bald man reached for the whip, turning to face Zeb.

"Grampa?" Zeb asked, taking a long, hard look. The man looked completely different without all that shaggy white hair…but it was his grampa, all right.

The old man frowned and stared. Zeb started to move back onto the bench, but the black man had his arm pressed hard against Zeb's chest.

"Zeb?" the old man cried. His voice quavered. "What are you doin' here? How did you get here?" He nodded to the black driver and helped Zeb back onto the bench. He held him at arm's length, staring at his face.

Zeb threw his arms around the old man. Tears were flowing down his cheeks. "Oh, Grampa," he sobbed. "I just knew you were alive! McPhee said you'd been killed by outlaws, but I didn't believe him…. I've found you! I've found you!"

"What?" The old man pulled away. "I wasn't shot by outlaws! *McPhee* was the one who shot me!"

CHAPTER EIGHT

Suba and Andy Disappear

October 14, 1811

Zeb relaxed his tight grip on his grampa's shoulder and wiped his sleeve across his face. *I want so much for Grampa to see me as a man, and here I am crying like a little kid.*

"Zeb, I still can't believe you're here, but I'm mighty glad to see you." He looked over at the man sitting on the other side of Zeb. "Walter, this is Zeb, my grandson!"

The black man nodded at Zeb. "Sorry about pushin' you so hard."

The old man put his arm around Zeb and hugged him. "So McPhee told you and your mama that I was shot and killed by outlaws?"

Zeb nodded. "We've gotta get home in a hurry, Grampa. McPhee told Mama that the farm belongs to him now, that you two had an agreement. Mama just went to pieces. I packed her up and took her in to Franklin to Uncle Ira and Aunt Annie. All the fight went out of her."

"Don't worry," the old man said. "I sent a letter by post rider almost two months ago to your Mama, and one to your uncle Ira, telling him what happened. I asked him to talk with the sheriff. By now McPhee and his men should be in jail."

"But Grampa, McPhee's men followed me down the trail a ways.... McPhee and his men might be in Natchez!"

"I haven't seen any of 'em yet, or heard they're in town, but we'll hafta be even more careful now," his grampa replied.

The old man looked around. "Where's Christmas?"

Before Zeb could answer, a small figure caught his eye.

Zeb had forgotten all about Hannah. She was walking alongside the wagon grinning up at him. His grampa noticed her at the same time. "You called to me earlier," he said to her. "How'd you know my name?"

Zeb reached across and offered his hand to Hannah. She climbed up and sat on the other side of the old man. "This is Hannah, Grampa, Hannah McAllister. I found her on the Natchez Road. We traveled together...." He paused. "I'd better tell you about that later."

He turned to face his grampa. "Christmas was exhausted. I had to leave him with the McAllisters. Hannah loaned me her horse, Suba." He paused, hating to have to tell him about Suba. "Mr. Moore and the sergeant have her," he said, pointing to the little tavern at the river edge. "They're still in there." He told his grampa what had happened to him that morning.

His grandfather narrowed his eyes as he looked at the tavern. "You're sayin' that Dancey Moore and the sergeant have your friend's horse, and a letter of authorization in your name? You didn't sign anything?"

Zeb shook his head. "I barely got out of there alive. Some big boatman, name of Lonnie Champ, who calls himself 'the cock of the walk', told 'em I was his partner, and they let me go. But they still have Suba. She may be long gone by now."

He slumped against the cotton bale. "Mr. Moore has Andy, too," he said. "I saw him tethered to the rail."

Zeb's grampa frowned. "So Dancey Moore has my horse," he said. "I should've guessed that!" He thought for a moment. "Zeb," he said, "normally, I'd insist that we plan this very carefully. I've been comin' down here every day or so for a month, lookin' for Andy. But if we're goin' to save Suba and get Andy back from Dancey Moore, we hafta move now."

"Please step down, Hannah, so I can get by." Grasping the bench rail with his right hand, he winced and lowered himself carefully to the ground.

"Come on, Zeb!" He turned as Hannah joined them. "Hannah, please wait here with Walter. I need you here to keep a lookout for Suba." Mr. Ryan called up to Walter. "Will you get the men to unload that wagon as quickly as possible? Then bring the horses and wagon up to that little tavern over there."

The black man nodded. Hannah climbed back up on the bench and sat next to him.

Zeb walked behind his grampa, marveling at the way the bald head and his clothing changed his appearance. *That's why he's not wearing a hat,* Zeb realized, *so people can see that bald head. He's still the same man: medium height, stocky, muscular, barrel-chested.*

Zeb had found his grampa. *But what's wrong with his left arm?* he wondered. *Good thing he's right-handed.*

As Zeb and his grampa hurried toward the little river-edge tavern, the old man told him that the tavern belonged to Dancey Moore. "I consider him to be the biggest rascal in the horse trading business. Gives all the rest of us a bad name."

They pushed open the heavy tavern door. At one end of the bar stood Lonnie Champ. The crowd of men seemed to be giving him as much room as he wanted. When he saw Zeb, he roared, "I told you to git, boy. I can't be responsible fer you in here. Dancey Moore and that sergeant'll be back any minute."

Zeb looked around the room. "But where'd they go?"

"Said they were gonna take care of a couple a' horses. Heard him tell the bartender they'd be back within the hour. You'd better git, boy. That sergeant may have a bad right hand, but he could easily kill ya with the other."

"Let's go," Zeb's grampa said. He motioned to Zeb, and they turned and hurried out of the tavern.

Outside they found the wagon being unloaded. When the last bale was rolled off, the old man asked Walter to drive it to the tavern and hitch the horses to the rail in the alley. Three other wagons were there, and more were at the other taverns. While the owners were inside getting a drink, the drivers waited outside, guarding the wagon and horses.

Zeb's grampa waved to Hannah. "Get into the wagon bed. Zeb, you climb up to the wagon bed, too," he said. "I'm goin' to talk to the constable. Then when Dancey Moore and the sergeant return, we'll find out where the horses are."

The black man leaned over. "I know what Mr. Moore looks like, Mr. Ryan. I'll keep an eye out up here."

About a half hour later, Walter turned around to where Zeb and Hannah were talking quietly in the bed of the wagon and said in a low voice, "Here comes your grampa now. You two had best keep your heads down."

The old man climbed into bed of the wagon. Zeb watched him struggle to climb up, using only his right hand. When they were all settled in the wagon, Zeb hugged his grampa again. "Did you talk with the constable?"

"No. He's out lookin' for you. And Hannah, I told your father that you're with us. I left a message with him for the constable."

Zeb's grampa wrapped his right arm around Zeb's shoulders and squeezed. "I'm surprised to see you, Zeb, but I'm glad you're here." He leaned back against the side of the wagon. "We've probably got as much as a half hour to wait." The old man rubbed the fuzz on his head.

Zeb watched him. "When did you shave your head?" he asked?

"This turned out to be the best disguise I could've had," his grampa said. "Nobody recognizes me. Passed right by Henry King. Known him for years. He didn't say a word. I've been stayin' with Culpepper on his horse breeding farm up in Washington."

"Culpepper!" Hannah whispered. "Suba stays at his farm. We were there yesterday."

"Suba must be a fine animal. Culpepper doesn't deal with anything but the best."

Hannah patted the wagon bed. "So this is the Culpepper wagon. I thought it looked like it."

"Shavin' my head was Culpepper's idea," the old man said. "Everybody knows me 'cause of all that white hair. With it shaved off, and wearin' these overalls, I was just another farmer."

Zeb's Grampa turned suddenly and grasped Zeb's arm. "That must've been *you* Culpepper was talkin' about. Said he met a young fellah with hair just like mine, who talked the way I do about horses. Said his family raised horses for the army. Not many doin' that. I never thought it could be you. There was no way you could be in Natchez."

"I heard he was comin' to talk to me at the McAllisters," Zeb said, "but I left for Natchez before he came. Wish he had said something to me when we met. If he had, I wouldn't be down here now, wouldn't have lost Suba."

"Don't worry, we'll get Suba back. They haven't had time to hide her far from here. And we'll get Andy, too."

Zeb looked up and down the length of the big wagon. "Why were you ridin' in this big cotton wagon? I've never seen one like this."

"It's a local copy of a Conestoga wagon, used for freight back East. Belongs to Mr. Culpepper, but these horses are *our* first-class draft horses. Culpepper already bred 'em with some of the draft horses he brought over from Ireland. I bought 'em the first day I arrived."

"You bought them?"

"I had funds. McPhee only got the money from the sale of the six horses. I keep most of our horse trading money in a local Natchez bank. The rest is up in the bank in Nashville."

"But why were you drivin' that load of cotton?"

"I needed a way to get into Natchez once or twice a week without bein' noticed. So I arranged with some plantation owners to bring their cotton into town."

"You needed to get into Natchez?"

"I knew I'd be more likely than the constable to spot Tate and his men. I also wanted to find Andy."

Zeb reached across and touched his grampa's left arm. The old man winced. "What happened to your arm, Grampa?"

"Nothin' to worry about," he said. "Hurt it when I fell off the horse and rolled down that bank. The doctor told me I'd dislocated my shoulder. He got the bone back in its socket, but it keeps comin' out. It's a bit painful. He told me to wear a sling and to lay off ridin' for a while, but I didn't want anyone to know about my arm, so I've taken the sling off."

"You fell off the horse? But when you said Tate McPhee shot you, I thought he wounded you in that arm. I'm surprised you're still alive."

"Bet McPhee will be, too. I suspected that McPhee and those men he had with him were plannin' something. So while they were sleepin' off a wild night in Natchez Under-the-Hill, I took the pistol balls out of their pistols and replaced 'em with paper wadding."

Zeb grinned. "Paper wadding?"

"When McPhee shot me, he was right behind me. He hit me with a wad of paper. The pistol made a loud noise and the horse reared. I went off the horse and down that steep riverbank, headed for the river."

"They didn't see you?"

"No. They must've chased Andy. He had the money belt, and he's a valuable horse. By the time they looked over the bank, I'd caught on to some bushes and was hidin' behind 'em. Must've thought I had gone into the river."

"So they don't know you're alive."

"If they've checked their guns and found the pistol balls are missing, they may be worried about whether I'm alive or dead."

"So McPhee and his men may feel they hafta finish the job. If they don't and you tell anybody what they did, they're in real trouble. Stealing horses is a hanging offense."

"That's why I wrote to Ira, and I hope at least McPhee is in jail. But you said he and his men may be here."

"If you do see 'em, what'll you do?"

"I have it all set up with the constable, just in case. He knows what happened, and he knows Tate McPhee."

He looked at Zeb and Hannah. "I'm really surprised that you made it all the way down the Natchez Road. I'm proud of you. Thank God you made it safely."

Hannah told Zeb's grampa about Zeb's being made an honorary Choctaw brave.

"Zeb, I'm very impressed. The Choctaw rarely make anyone an honorary member of their tribe. That's quite an honor." He looked at Zeb proudly for a few moments before he spoke again. "Zeb, earlier you said you found Hannah on the highway?"

Hannah piped up, her face grim. "I was kidnapped by an outlaw gang, what's left of the Mason gang. They used me as bait on the highway. I was supposed to stand on the highway and say, 'Please, mister, I'm lost.' If the traveler stopped, the outlaws would rob him."

"That must've been terrible, Hannah. But how did you escape from the gang? How did you and Zeb meet? And how did you come down the Natchez Road?"

"Well," Hannah replied slowly, "when the outlaws went north to try to steal a bunch of money, I hid. I had planned it for a long time. I was still hiding when I met up with Zeb."

She grinned at Zeb. They both began to talk, telling and remembering, correcting each other and laughing at the different ways they recalled what had happened. They told him about two of Tate McPhee's men, Big Red and the Fiddler, following Zeb that first night. They talked about crossing the violent, swollen Duck River, doubting they would survive. They told him about the outlaws who tried to stop them. If it hadn't been for Hannah's warning and her whacking the man on the shoulder with her club, they probably would have been caught. They told him about the bet with the sergeant and the sergeant's vow to have revenge.

"If I hadn't made that bet with the sergeant," Zeb said, "and then kinda rubbed his nose in it, we wouldn't have him as an enemy."

"Rubbed his nose in it?"

"He wanted to bet me ten dollars I couldn't stay on Harlequin for five minutes, bareback. I bet him the horse against everything I had."

"The horse? You didn't bet Christmas!"

"No. I bet my rifle and saddle and the two old pistols against Harlequin. And I won."

"So he's your enemy because he bet and lost?"

"It wasn't only for that. At first, I thought the soldiers, who were dressed in dirty old clothes, were outlaws and that they had killed you and stolen the horses. I called 'em yellow-bellied cowards. That's all he seems to remember about me."

Hannah wouldn't let it go at that. "I think you were very brave. You called them those names, trying to keep all of their attention on you, so I could run away."

Zeb looked at her soberly. "The sergeant is still after me. He tried to kill me in that tavern, but Lonnie Champ, a big flatboat man, told him I was his partner. The sergeant backed off, for now."

The old man turned to Zeb. "How did the sergeant steal Hannah's horse?"

Zeb sighed. "It was my fault. I knew that Mr. Moore was interested in her. He offered me a thousand dollars for her."

"A thousand dollars for a horse he'd never seen before? Doesn't sound like Dancey Moore."

Zeb hated having to tell Hannah what he had done. "He knew how valuable Suba is. Everybody does," Zeb said, looking at his hands. "I raced her last night down here in Natchez Under-The-Hill."

"You raced Suba?" Hannah cried. "Oh, Zeb, she might've gotten hurt."

Zeb's grampa nodded. "I'm surprised you did that, Zeb."

"I know," Zeb said, looking up at Hannah. "I was runnin' out of money…but it was the wrong thing to do. I'm sorry, Hannah."

"Is she all right?"

"She's fine! She won first place, even against a Natchez racehorse."

64

"First place!" Hannah exclaimed.

"She really is fast, Hannah. She takes to racin' the way Christmas does."

"Then the sergeant stole her to sell to Dancey Moore."

"I should never have ridden her down here this morning when I was lookin' for Grampa. Dancey Moore had told me he'd be here.... Then the sergeant showed up and swore out a warrant for my arrest. Said that I had kidnapped Hannah."

"Kidnapped?"

Zeb nodded. "Nothin' I could say would convince the constable. And when the constable arrested me and threw me into jail, the sergeant stole Suba."

Zeb's grampa slowly shook his head. Then he turned to Hannah. "How'd your father find out that Zeb was in jail?"

"He didn't know about that. He came down to talk with the constable about McPhee and the sergeant and to see if Zeb needed any help finding you."

Walter interrupted. "Mr. Ryan, here come two men on horseback. One of 'em looks like Mr. Moore."

Zeb's grampa peeked over the edge of the wagon. "That's Moore, all right. Must be the sergeant with him. Looks like they're headed for the tavern. We'll wait a few minutes, give 'em a chance to get settled."

How will Grampa be able to force Dancey Moore and the sergeant to give up the horses? Zeb wondered. *I always thought of Grampa as invincible. But now, with his bad shoulder....*

Grampa nudged him. "Let's go, Zeb." He turned to Hannah. "You stay here. I need you and Walter to watch the back door. If they come out, watch where they go."

When they walked into the tavern, Lonnie Champ looked up and shouted, "I told you to stay out of here, boy. This aint no place for you."

Zeb's grampa ignored him. He walked over to the table where the sergeant and Dancey Moore were seated. "I want those two horses now, and I want the papers for Suba."

The sergeant reached for his pistol. Cracker Ryan stepped back and, in one fluid motion, snaked his whip out with a terrible explosive crack. It snapped the pistol out of the sergeant's hand and slammed it on the floor. "The next time," he said, "it may be your hand lyin' there on the floor."

He turned to the other man. "Moore, do you want to try for your gun, too?"

Dancey Moore cursed under his breath, putting his hands flat on the table.

The old man demanded again, "All right, where are those horses?"

Dancey Moore snarled, "There's no way yer gonna get that black horse. I got her from the sergeant here. How he got her is none of my business. And I bought your horse from Tate McPhee, fair and square. Got the papers to prove it. He's legally mine. I've got 'em both now, and you'll never find 'em."

The old man stepped back again and snapped the whip next to Dancey Moore's hand, taking a chip of wood out of the heavy oak table.

Dancey Moore whispered something to the sergeant.

"All right. All right," the sergeant said, glaring at Zeb and his grampa. "We'll tell you where the horses are." Moore and the sergeant stood up.

Zeb and his grampa moved closer to the table. Dancey Moore shouted, "*Now!*"

He and the sergeant flipped the heavy table over. Zeb shoved his grampa aside and jumped back. The heavy table landed where Zeb and his grampa had been standing. Moore

Cracker Ryan snaked his whip out with a terrible
explosive crack.

and the sergeant ducked through a low door hidden behind the bar. "C'mon, Grampa, let's go after them."

Lonnie Champ shouted, "No! That's what they wantcha to do. They're probably waitin' fer ya jes outside the door."

Zeb's grampa nodded. "He's right."

Lonnie Champ said, "I know who you are, sir. Yer Cracker Ryan. I ain't never seen no one handle a whip like that. I sure would like to learn how to do it."

Zeb looked around the room. "What are we gonna do, Grampa?"

"First, Zeb, we'll try the law again." He nodded to Lonnie Champ as they stepped out onto the rickety porch, then turned to Zeb. "I'm goin' to speak to the police constable. He should be back by now. You get up in the wagon and watch. Silver Street's the only road out of Natchez Under-the-Hill, so keep your eye on that road. I'll be right back."

Zeb climbed back into the wagon. He told Hannah what had happened. They waited quietly, listening to the music and bursts of laughter coming from the taverns. Zeb looked at Hannah and they both smiled. In a way, it was just like so many days they spent on the Natchez Road, sitting quietly together, hidden in the forest, waiting for travelers to go by.

Suddenly, the driver called down to them, "A horse wrangler just ran out of the tavern and jumped on his horse! He's gallopin' up the road to Natchez."

CHAPTER NINE

The Standoff

October 14, 1811

Z eb bolted upright. "I bet they sent that man to move the horses! And I bet I know where he's going...." He looked at Hannah. "I'm gonna need your horse."

Hannah was staring across the big river. She looked so sad. Zeb hated himself for putting her prized horse in jeopardy.

"I rode Christmas down here, Zeb," she said a low voice. She pointed toward the rail at the jailhouse. "He's around the corner of the jail."

Zeb jumped off the wagon and put his hand up to help Hannah down. "C'mon," he called up to her. "You can go to the jailhouse to be with Grampa and your father."

Zeb and Hannah ran down the street toward the jail. "I'll get her back for you, Hannah," he said, "I promise."

When they reached Christmas, Hannah went into the jailhouse. Zeb swung himself up on the big horse and trotted quickly through the crowds toward Silver Street. He shouted to Walter as he passed, "Let Grampa know I've gone to the Texada Inn!"

Zeb turned the horse up the cobblestone road, still jammed with cotton wagons and men on foot, all moving toward the docks. Christmas sensed the urgency, forcing his big body through the crowd without slowing down. The rapid *clang*

clang of iron horseshoes against the cobblestones rang out a warning to all pedestrians in the way. Men shouted and cursed at Zeb, shaking their fists.

When Zeb got to the top of Silver Street, the number of cotton wagons had thinned out. He ran Christmas at full gallop up Washington Street to the Texada Tavern.

Zeb rode through a crowd of men on foot, into the stable yard. One of the men, barely jumping out of the way in time, shouted up to Zeb, "Watch what yer doin'!"

Zeb pulled the big horse up, but Christmas pivoted, scattering the men even more. At that moment, one of Dancey Moore's horse wranglers, the one who had told him about the old man with the whip, came out of the stables. Seated on an Indian pony, the man was leading Suba on one side of him and Andy on the other. Both horses were tacked up, ready to be ridden away. When the wrangler saw Zeb, he dropped Andy's lead line and reached for a pistol stuck in his belt. "Let me by!" he shouted.

Christmas was still skittering. But Zeb had spent many hours on Christmas at the family farm, rounding up the horses and cutting some out from the herd for branding. And all of the horses on his grampa's farm were trained to move mostly with leg and seat signals so the arms were free for shooting a musket or for working. The reins were only used to help stop the horse. As Zeb leaned in the direction of the wrangler, Christmas immediately moved sideways toward the man, crowding him and his horse against the stable wall.

The wrangler backed his horse, pulling hard on the reins with his other hand. "Let me by," he said, "or I'll shoot you." He waved the pistol, then cocked it and snarled, "Move out of the way!"

The men in the stable yard backed even further away.

Zeb gulped, looking down the barrel of the gun. He tried to think about what his grampa would do. He knew that Grampa had told him to watch for the men and then to wait for him. *But if I back away now,* he thought, *we'll probably never see those horses again.*

He put his hands in the air and took a deep breath, forcing himself to relax and smile confidently. "You gonna shoot an unarmed man in front of all these witnesses? They already know you're a horse thief, and you know what the penalty is for that."

The wrangler looked down the road. Zeb could hear a horse galloping in their direction and, in the distance, the fast *clop clop* and the metallic grinding sound of four horses pulling a heavy wagon. Zeb kept Christmas moving sideways.

Christmas forced the wrangler's horse against the stable door. "Looks like we've got some extra witnesses," Zeb said, his hands still in the air. "This may be your last chance."

The wrangler glared at Zeb. "Yer crazy as that old coot!" he growled. He dropped Suba's reins, turned, and galloped away on his horse.

Zeb moved Christmas to where Andy was standing near the gate. He leaned over and grabbed Andy's reins just as Hannah arrived on her father's horse.

"Suba!" Hannah exclaimed. The black horse stood nervously in the middle of the stable yard, pawing the ground, ready to bolt. Hannah lowered her voice. "Easy, girl. It's all right." She eased her mount closer to Suba, talking quietly as she leaned over and picked up the dragging reins from the ground.

She hopped off her father's horse and put her arms around Suba's neck. "Oh, Suba," she whispered, "I'm so glad to see you." She checked the horse's mouth and then ran her hands over the horse's flanks and belly. She ran her hands up and down the horse's legs. "Are you all right, Suba? Did they hurt you?"

As Hannah was checking Suba, the cotton wagon turned into the stable yard. Walter was driving the team. Dr. McAllister and Grampa stood behind him, holding on to the bench. Grampa had his whip in his hand.

"Zeb!" the old man cried out with relief. "I thought you were a goner! I saw you with your hands up." Cracker Ryan slapped the coiled whip nervously against his leg. "I was just hopin' we'd get here before it was too late. He looked down the road where the wrangler had gone. "I thought you might need some help. Looks like I was wrong."

He held on to the back of the bench for support, then smiled down at Zeb. "See you found both horses."

"Yup. They seem to be all right."

As Hannah mounted Suba and started to walk her around the yard, Zeb's grampa climbed down carefully from the wagon. He checked Andy and started to tighten the saddle girth, but he couldn't do it one-handed. Zeb tightened the girth and then gave his grampa a leg up. He watched him settle painfully and awkwardly into the saddle. Zeb shook his head slightly. *He can't use that arm at all.*

Zeb's grampa looked at him and nodded. "It's not much good to me these days," he said.

The old man turned and looked at the others. "We can't stay here. This is where Dancey Moore stays when he's in town. Let's get over to King's Tavern," he said. "We can talk there."

They rode to King's Tavern and entered the stable yard. Mr. King came out, shouting at them. "I've told you men before! I don't have any room until after the cotton harvest. You can eat here, but you can't leave the horses back there. The stables are for the guests only."

Zeb's grampa halted near Mr. King and looked down at him. "Henry," he said quietly, "it's Daniel Ryan."

Zeb clucked Christmas forward so he was alongside his grampa. Mr. King looked at one and then the other and then chuckled. "I never would have recognized you with that bald head, Cracker."

"It's a long story, old friend. I promise to tell you all about it later. We'll just be here a few hours. But we'd like to keep the horses in the stables if we can, with our driver and one or two of your people keepin' watch. Do you mind askin' 'em to let us know immediately if Dancey Moore or some of his men show up?"

"Not at all, Cracker. Always pleased to have you."

Cracker Ryan paused for a moment. "And, Henry, please let us know if anyone sees Tate McPhee."

Mr. King shook his head. "He's a dangerous one, McPhee is. My men will look out for him. But what makes you think he's here?"

"Zeb spotted two of McPhee's men following him on the Natchez Road. They may have passed him when he was off the trail for a few days."

Zeb slipped off Christmas and then helped his grampa dismount. The old man gingerly picked up his left hand with his right and tucked it back into the bib of his overalls.

Zeb's grampa put his right arm around Zeb's shoulders as they made their way through the door of King's Tavern together. The group gathered around a large table in a corner of the room; everyone seemed to be talking at once. Mr. King came over with a pot of coffee and pewter mugs. Zeb's grampa stood behind a chair and said, "Let us pray."

He bowed his head, paused for a moment, and then began, "Father in heaven, we thank thee for all the blessings of this life. We thank thee for the good friends we've made on the way to Natchez and here in Natchez, who have played such an important part in all of this..... Bless this food to our use and us to thy service. Amen."

Dr. McAllister, seated to the left of Zeb's grampa, murmured, "Amen." He turned to face the old man. "I hope," he said, "that you're not planning to travel anytime soon. Let me take a look at that arm."

"But we have to get back to Franklin!" Zeb's grampa protested.

The doctor lifted the arm and touched and prodded. "I'm sure you know that you have had a severe dislocation of the humerus. When did this happen?"

"More'n two months ago."

The doctor shook his head. "It would be almost healed by now if it had been immobilized. It won't heal if you keep moving it, Mr. Ryan. You really shouldn't be riding with it or it might become a chronic condition."

"I know," the old man said. "It seems to be gettin' worse. The doctor I saw put my arm in a sling, but I'm afraid I took it off."

Dr. McAllister lowered the arm gently to the table. "I'll put a sling on it before we leave here. You'll have to keep it immobile for at least another six weeks, maybe longer."

Mr. King and two helpers came out of the kitchen with rice, fried plantain, and a pot of okra, sausage, and hot spicy fish and crawfish.

Hannah looked up at Zeb. "I hope you do stay at least six weeks, Zeb," she said in a quiet voice.

A long, narrow loaf of hard-crusted bread was plopped on the table near Hannah. Zeb looked at her just as she turned to look up at him. He knew that she too was remembering that first night they met on the on the Natchez Road. When he found her, she was starving. She had stolen the loaf of bread he had brought from home, and before long, had eaten almost all of it.

74

"We keep eatin' like this," Zeb whispered in his best Kaintuck accent, "we'uns won't wanna go back."

Zeb's grampa motioned to Mr. King. "Please make sure that the wagon driver is well fed."

"I've already sent bowls of food out to him and the two men out there with him."

Zeb's grampa served himself as the food was passed around. "So who's takin' care of the farm, Zeb?"

"Josh and the two boys are stayin' at the farm. They can do all the daily chores till we get home."

"But Ira needs Josh at the print shop."

Zeb shook his head, chewed, and swallowed. "Uncle Ira said he's given up on Josh working in the print shop. Josh loves the farm, and he isn't interested at all in the newspaper."

"So Ira knew you were goin' to travel down the Natchez Road?"

"No, I didn't tell Uncle Ira. I hated to lie to him, so I just told him I was gonna need help on the farm for a while."

Zeb looked away. "I worry about Mama. When I left, she was holdin' her little bundle of clothes pressed against her chest, rockin' in the chair. She thinks we've lost the farm."

"My letter should help. She knows I'm alive. And Ira will help her understand we haven't lost the farm. I just hope Josh hasn't had to tangle with McPhee or his men."

Mr. King returned to the table and handed the old man a folded sheet of paper sealed with a glob of red wax. "Post rider was just here with the mail," he said. "Had a letter for you. He had to get to the fort in New Orleans in a hurry, Cracker. Told me to tell you he'll be back in a week, heading north."

Mr. King turned toward Zeb. "He'll pick up that letter you gave me on his way back."

The old man smiled. "A letter to your mama?"

Zeb nodded.

"This one's from her. I'd know her handwriting anywhere."

The old man pulled out a coin purse and dropped two coins in Mr. King's hands. "Is that still the tariff for one page?" he asked.

Mr. King nodded and returned to the front desk.

The old man sat down. He opened the letter and he and Zeb read it together.

Dear Daddy,

I was so glad to hear from you. Thank the good Lord you're still alive. Tate said you were killed by outlaws. He said the farm was his now, that you two had an agreement. Ira says he's sure that's a lie.

I have real sad news for you. Zeb is somewhere on the road to Natchez looking for you. I doubt he's still alive. I don't know if I can stand it, losing him, too. First it was Zeb's daddy, then it was you, and now Zeb. I know he must have felt that he had to go. If only he had waited a few days. He would have seen your letter.

Please come home soon. You're all I've got now.

Love, Alice

Zeb closed his eyes, holding back his tears from having caused her so much pain. *I knew she wouldn't have wanted me to leave,* he thought, *but I never thought of how painful it'd be for her, thinking that Daddy, then Grampa, and then I were all dead.*

The old man patted Zeb's shoulder. "You did what you felt you had to do. If you'd been a few years older, she would've expected you to come down the trail. Your mama will be fine once she gets a letter from the two of us."

He smiled at Zeb. "You must know that I'm glad you're here, Zeb. But we're goin' to hafta be vigilant if we're gonna spend six weeks or more here in Natchez. Tate McPhee wants us dead, and it looks like Dancey Moore and the sergeant'll spend the rest of their lives tryin' to get even."

The old man looked at him for a long moment. He pushed back his chair and got to his feet. "Zeb," he said. "Stand up, boy."

Zeb stood tall next to him. They were the same height now. The old man grasped Zeb's shoulder with his right hand. "You've gotten a lot taller. Put on some muscle, too."

He cleared his throat. "You've also grown in a lot of other, more important ways. The Choctaw must've seen what I'm seein' now." He paused. "I'll be glad to have another man with me on the way back up the Natchez Road."

He clapped Zeb on the shoulder. "When we get back tonight, I'll see if John Culpepper has someplace for you to sleep. You could always stay in my room over there, but it's pretty small...."

Dr. McAllister interrupted. "That's all taken care of, Mr. Ryan. Martha and I want Zebulon to stay with us. We have a bedroom all made up and ready for him. We're not far from Culpepper's place."

CHAPTER TEN

Captain Morrison

October 15, 1811

When Zeb awoke the next morning at the McAllister house, he dressed quickly, walked barefoot across the wood plank floor through the house to the back door, sat on the porch steps, and put on his boots.

He lifted his head and sniffed. Something was cooking in the kitchen. He went out to the privy and then washed his hands and face at the pump.

In the kitchen he found Dr. McAllister and Sarah.

"Well, Zeb, you're up early." The doctor sniffed the aroma of Sarah's cooking. "I'm hungry, Sarah," he said. "Hungry for the first time in a long time."

Tears welled up in Sarah's eyes. "Why don't you two go into the dining room and I'll serve you some eggs and grits, biscuits, and maybe a little white gravy," she said.

They had just finished breakfast when Sarah came in again. "Doctor," she whispered, "there are two soldiers in the back-yard. They want to talk with Miz Hannah."

Dr. McAllister frowned, throwing his napkin on the table and pushing back his chair. "I can't imagine who that could be. What could they want at this hour? Who could know that Hannah is home?"

Zeb got up, too. "I think I may know who it is," he said.

An army officer and a sergeant were in the backyard, dressed in the uniforms of the Mounted Light Dragoons. They had dismounted and were leading their horses.

When Hannah's father opened the door and stepped out onto the back porch, the officer came to attention. He saluted and then said, "Dr. McAllister?"

"I am Dr. McAllister. Who are you, and what do you want with Hannah?"

"Please excuse the early hour," the captain said. "We have a lot to do today."

At that moment, Hannah burst out of the house. She had obviously dressed in a hurry, as she was wearing the same clothes she had worn the day before. "Captain Morrison!" she cried. "How did you find us?"

"Hello, Hannah. You weren't hard to find. There is only one Dr. McAllister in Washington. I came to thank you for telling us what the outlaws were planning when you left them—"

"Did you get to Franklin in time to stop them?"

"Yes, we did. They would have robbed the army payroll, but we were able to escort the men with the money to Fort Dearborn without incident. The Mason gang must have heard us on the trail, because they never showed up."

Hannah shivered. "I wonder what happened to them."

Captain Morrison flicked his hand as if brushing away a fly. "It doesn't matter. They probably just fled into the woods...."

Hannah shook her head. "They said that after that big robbery they were gonna come down here to Natchez to live."

"Don't worry," the captain said. "We'll keep an eye out for them. I came here today to tell you and your family how much we appreciated your help."

He turned to Zeb. "Did you find your grandfather?"

"Yes sir, I did…but we'd like to keep that quiet. There are some dangerous men after him."

"I understand. But I have some news for both of you. I'd like to see him right away."

Hannah and Zeb mounted horses and led the way to the Culpepper farm. It was still very early in the morning, and the group found Mr. Culpepper and Katie eating breakfast.

"Captain Morrison and his sergeant have something urgent to discuss with Grampa," Zeb said. "I'll go up and get him."

"I'll go talk with them for a moment," Mr. Culpepper said.

When Zeb got up to the room, his grampa was sitting on the edge of the bed. "Captain Morrison wants to see you, Grampa," Zeb said. "Says he has some important news for you. They just came down from Franklin, so maybe it has something to do with Mama or the farm."

Captain Morrison was sitting on the porch with Mr. Culpepper. "I don't see any problem," Mr. Culpepper was saying. "If you can't use Fort Dearborn for your staging area, why not let them come here? I have forty acres lying fallow just beyond that fence. See that little hill in the back? On the other side of that is a wide creek with good, clear water, just the place to set up camp for you and your men and for those who want to go north with you."

"Thank you. That will be very helpful," the captain said. "My patrol will set up camp here a week before we leave. The civilians who will be going with us must camp here also, and they must be ready to leave with no more than a day's notice."

When Captain Morrison saw Zeb's grampa, he got up and saluted him. "Good morning, Mr. Ryan."

The old man shook his hand. "Good morning, Captain. I understand you have an urgent message for me."

"Yes, sir. I do. Please, let's sit down."

When they were seated, the captain continued. "Zeb had told us about Tate McPhee, so when we were in Franklin, we stopped by the sheriff's office. The sheriff had already tried to arrest McPhee, but when he got to the farm, McPhee and his men were gone. Your grandnephew Josh and his brothers were there, but they couldn't stop McPhee."

Captain Morrison told of how McPhee had taken all the horses, brood stock, everything, and killed the cow.

Zeb groaned. *We are left with almost nothing.*

"And Alice, Zeb's mama?" Cracker Ryan asked.

"She's all right and back on the farm. Josh is there workin' with her."

Zeb sighed with relief. "What happened to McPhee and his men?" he asked. "Are they headed this way?"

"No. They headed west, toward Memphis, selling the horses as they traveled. Unfortunately, they crossed the Mississippi and are now in the town of New Madrid. The county sheriff has no jurisdiction in that territory."

"Think they'll stay there?" Zeb's grampa asked.

The captain nodded. "I think so. The sheriff suspects they will use that base to start piracy on the river."

"Why New Madrid?"

"It's become a haven for outlaws. They'll be safe until the army decides to send a force over there."

The captain continued. "Mr. Ryan, I was just telling Mr. Culpepper that I shall be leading a patrol north in the next couple of months. I have been directed by the army to escort any civilians who wish to travel with us. We'll be leaving sometime in early December. You are welcome to go with us."

Zeb's grampa sat back and smiled. "That would solve our problem of gettin' back. We have four settled draft horses to take north. I wasn't sure how I'd do it."

"It would probably be impossible without an escort. The outlaws are becoming increasingly dangerous. Some of the gangs are even large enough to challenge groups of well-armed men traveling on the Nashville Road."

The old man nodded. "Your patrol will make all the difference."

"I will place information about the escort in the *Weekly Chronicle.* It comes out day after tomorrow, so we may get some response in the next few days."

Mr. Culpepper and Zeb's grampa stood up as Captain Morrison got to his feet.

Captain Morrison touched his helmet with his right hand. "I will send you a written agreement. I hope you won't mind that while we are using the pasture as a staging area it will be army property. That is done to help protect your property and the people who will be going with us."

"Just as long as you make it clear that it's only temporary. I plan to put those forty acres back into hay come spring."

Captain Morrison mounted his horse. "We should be gone," he said, "by mid-December. Thank you once again for your cooperation."

He touched the rim of his helmet and then he and the sergeant cantered down the long Culpepper driveway to the highway, heading for Fort Dearborn.

CHAPTER ELEVEN

Horseplay

October 16, 1811

Every day Zeb and Hannah rode over to the Culpepper farm. Hannah's mother often went with them. When she did, she sat on the Culpeppers' back porch and sewed.

Zeb, Hannah, and Katie exercised the horses each day, rain or shine. During heavy rainstorms, they worked the horses in the big barn.

In the late afternoons, when Zeb, Hannah, and Hannah's mother returned to the McAllister house, Dr. McAllister often invited Zeb into the laboratory, where he showed Zeb how he was trying to develop a means of preventing smallpox.

Zeb asked many questions about serums, cowpox, and vaccines. On the second day with Dr. McAllister, he shook his head. "It's all beyond me."

"No, it isn't. You have a good mind, Zeb. The Jefferson School, the one Nashoba was visiting, would be an excellent place for you to get more education."

While Zeb met with Dr. McAllister, Hannah sat at the kitchen table and wrote in the leather-bound notebook Zeb had given to her.

Zeb's uncle Ira had given Zeb two of the leather-bound books back home. While they were traveling down the Natchez

Road, Hannah had showed so much interest in writing that Zeb had given her one of the books and his pencil.

She had written in the book almost every day as they traveled down the Natchez Road, but she made Zeb promise never to read it. It appeared to Zeb that after little more than a month she was at least halfway through the notebook.

~

One day when Zeb had ridden from the McAllisters to the Culpepper farm to work with Kapucha, the Choctaw pony he had gentled in Yowani, a family arrived in an open farm wagon. The wheels wobbled on worn axles, squeaking in protest. An old horse, plodding slowly with his head down, pulled the wagon, his body wet with the effort.

Zeb's grampa, who had been sitting on the porch, stood up to greet them just as Mr. Culpepper trotted his horse up to the wagon.

Mr. Culpepper pulled his horse in and swung down off the saddle. He walked over to where the missionary was standing and held out his hand. "I'm John Culpepper. You folks planning to go north with the patrol?"

The man nodded. "I'm David Lodge," he said. "We hope to go with them as far as Yowani."

Mr. Culpepper pointed toward the lower forty acres. "The army patrol is using my back pasture as a staging area. You may camp down there."

Mr. Culpepper walked around the wagon, pulling on the wheel and looking at the undercarriage. He was shaking his head as he headed back to where Mr. Lodge was standing. "I hope you won't mind my being frank, sir, but that wagon will never make a trip on the Nashville Road as far as Yowani." He patted the horse's neck. "This horse won't make it, either. Should have been put out to pasture a long time ago."

Mr. Lodge looked back at the wagon and the poor little horse. "Mr. Moore, the man we bought it from, said it would get us to Yowani. He said it was the best he could do for the money we had."

"You had better deal with someone else."

The man's two little girls had climbed down and were twined around his legs. He patted them on their heads. "We can't," he said. "We don't have any more money."

"What are you going to live on?"

"I will try to do a little tutoring while we are waiting to leave."

"Tutoring? How much education do you have?"

"College and then seminary. I am a minister with the Presbyterian Church. I plan to go to Yowani as a missionary."

Culpepper grinned. "Seminary, and you've had a college education as well. We may just be able to give you all the students you need for the next couple of months. My daughter and her friend had been taking lessons here, but their teacher has gone back East. And there are four other girls their ages who took lessons with them."

"That would be wonderful," the missionary said. He exhaled as if a huge weight had been lifted from his shoulders.

Zeb walked over to them as Mr. Lodge reached up and helped his tall, slim wife step down from the wagon. *Her dress,* Zeb thought, *looks like one of the fine dresses I've seen ladies wear in Natchez.*

"This is my wife, Ruth." He put his hand on the head of the eldest girl. "This is Mary, and this little one is Beth."

"I am delighted to meet you," Mr. Culpepper said. "This is Zebulon D'Evereux." He gestured up to the porch. "And that is Zeb's grampa, Daniel Ryan."

85

The old man, his left arm in a sling, stepped down from the porch. He shook hands with the missionary and nodded his head to Mrs. Lodge. "Pleased to meet you. Looks like we'll be travelin' together."

The missionary smiled. "You're going to Yowani, too?"

"To Yowani and beyond, all the way to Franklin, just a few miles this side of Nashville. I look forward to travelin' with you."

Zeb's grampa patted the little horse. "Mr. Culpepper is right, sir," he said. "This horse couldn't possibly make the trip. But we can loan you one of our draft horses," the old man suggested. "You'd be doin' us a favor. If you don't use her, we'll hafta lead her."

"You really wouldn't mind?…"

"I wish you'd accept our offer, Mr. Lodge."

While Mr. Culpepper and Zeb's grampa talked with the Lodges, Zeb looked into the wagon bed, where he saw two canvas bags and a small wooden box. Nothing else. No canvas. No bedrolls.

"Where will you stay while you're waiting for the convoy to leave?" Culpepper asked Mr. Lodge.

"We thought we'd stay in the wagon. Get used to what it will be like on the trail."

Culpepper stroked his chin. "It's getting colder at night now, and there is a good possibility of rain tonight." He pointed to a little cottage next to the horse barns. "Since you'll be tutoring here, why don't you stay in the foreman's house? He moved west into the new territory to start his own horse ranch. It's empty until I find someone to take his place."

～

On the first day of the six girls' morning classes, Zeb, Hannah, and Mrs. McAllister rode over to the Culpepper place together. The missionary's wife, Mary Lodge, joined Hannah's mother on the porch. They sewed and talked and watched their children. *Hannah's mother must hate to let Hannah out of her sight, even for a moment,* Zeb thought. *But she knows that she can't keep her a prisoner in her own house.*

When it was time for the noon meal, four girls returned to Washington. Zeb noticed that even though Hannah had talked fondly of these girls, he never saw them being very friendly to Hannah and Katie. *Maybe they are jealous of Hannah and Katie's friendship or something silly like that,* he thought.

In the early afternoon, Katie and Hannah exercised the Culpepper horses and those being boarded there. In addition to Christmas and Kapucha, Zeb rode each of the draft horses to keep them in shape for the long trip north. Sometimes the missionary joined him, riding the mare that was going to pull their wagon.

Once the chores were done, Zeb discovered that Hannah and Katie were as competitive as he was. They raced Christmas and Suba and Katie's favorite gelding. They even invented races, and that is where the trouble started.

One day Katie proposed a different kind of race. They were sitting on the fence rail just after the noon meal. "Why don't we each run to our horses, tack up, and then move them to the paddock and out on the oval. We can gallop once around the oval. Whoever gets back to the paddock first wins."

They ran into the barn. Zeb was throwing his saddle on Christmas when he heard Hannah cry out, "Oh, no!"

"What is it?"

"She took the box I need to stand on to saddle Suba!"

Hannah grabbed an empty bucket, flipped it over, stood on it, and finished saddling Suba. She and Zeb quickly led the horses out of the barn. But by then Katie was already coming around the far end of the oval. She rode over to them and grinned. "You two sure are slow," she said.

That afternoon, when Hannah was exercising Harlequin, she rode him over to the rail where Katie and Zeb were sitting. "Want to try him out?" she asked Katie.

Katie shrugged. "Sure," she said. She hopped down off the rail. Hannah slipped off Harlequin. She held the cantle of the saddle. "Want me to hold him while you mount?"

"For heaven's sakes, Hannah. I can mount without your help."

Katie swung up onto the horse. The little horse started to twist and turn, jumping sideways and hopping around. Katie sat him easily. She smiled at Hannah and Zeb and sat back in the saddle. Suddenly the horse began to buck. Katie had to make an emergency dismount before she was thrown to the ground.

Hannah ran to Harlequin and grabbed the reins. She stroked his neck and then went around to the right side and adjusted the saddle pad. She slapped her hand against her pants and then mounted Harlequin and rode him back to the fence.

Katie was standing with her hands on her hips. "That horse is crazy. What did you do?"

She stepped closer and stared at Hannah's pants.

"Burrs!" she shouted. "You put burrs under the saddle while I mounted!"

When Katie saw the sly grin on Hannah's face, she relaxed and smiled. "All right. All right. You win," she said. "No more tricks."

CHAPTER TWELVE

The Sail Maker

October 25, 1811

A week after the missionary family arrived, Zeb was sitting with the McAllisters at the supper table. He was telling them about some of the strange people who had come out to the Culpeppers' to talk with the captain about going north with the patrol. A number of merchants arrived at the staging site with armed guards they had recruited from among the boaters down at the docks. Captain Morrison told them that the gold coins they were carrying would be an enormous temptation to men who owed them no loyalty. In spite of the warning, the merchants were usually too impatient for a six-week to two-month wait. They would leave the next morning to head north on the Nashville Road. Captain Morrison doubted they'd ever be seen again.

Zeb told them that Kaintucks heading north on foot now stopped to gather at the Culpepper place until they had at least twenty-five men. They sometimes talked, almost wistfully, about going with the patrol, but it was only possible for those going on horseback.

"I need to do some things in Natchez tomorrow morning," Zeb said finally. "Is there anything I can get for you while I'm there?"

"I'd like to go with you, Zeb, if you don't mind," Hannah said. "Mama wants me to talk with Miss Phillipa about having some town clothes made." She made a funny grimace. "Can you imagine? She wants to know what girls my age are wearing, and I'm s'posed to bring home some fabric samples from Foley's General Store."

"It's time for you to dress the way other girls do," her mother said.

"I know. I'll do it," Hannah groaned. "I just think it's funny. With my short hair I'll look like a boy in his sister's clothes."

"Your hair is already growing back. You'll look fine."

Hannah fingered her hair. "They cut it about a week before I met Zeb. They thought I looked too Choctaw, so Elizabeth, one of the Mason gang women, took some sheep shears and chopped off the braid. When she tried to even it up, she made it worse. She said it was my fault because I kept yelling and screaming and I wouldn't hold still."

Zeb remembered the red switch marks on the backs of her legs. *That's probably how they finally forced her to let them cut it. There is so much she will probably never tell her mother.*

That evening after supper, Hannah's mother sat in her rocker and sewed. Zeb and Dr. McAllister headed to the laboratory, and Hannah sat at the kitchen table, writing in her diary with a quill, rather than the pencil she had used on the road.

"You musta had lot happen today, Miz Hannah," Zeb heard Sarah observe, "for you to be writin' so much tonight."

"It isn't what happened today, Sarah," Hannah said. "Something Mama said brought back memories that I want to put down in my diary."

∼

The next morning Zeb and Hannah left for Natchez.

Zeb hoped no one would recognize him. His hair was cut short—Hannah had seen to that—and he wore his grampa's broad-brimmed hat. He was now wearing town clothes and a pair of dress boots. They were hand-me-downs, borrowed from Katie Culpepper's brother, Sean, who had gone East to college.

He was riding Maggie, a small horse he had borrowed from Mr. Culpepper. Hannah was riding one of the Culpepper's ponies. She wore some of the boy's clothes she had brought from Yowani. They headed to Natchez, laughing at each other.

They paid the toll and crossed the bridge at Catherine Creek on the outskirts of the city. Then they continued on Jefferson Street.

Zeb thought of all he and his grampa had talked about as they had planned the trip back to Franklin. He looked up. Hannah was watching him, but she didn't say anything. They had always respected each other's silences on the trail. He smiled. "Sorry," he said. "I was thinkin' about all I hafta do."

"Me, too," Hannah said. "I keep thinkin' about how much I like it here, and then I think of Yowani. Life is so different here."

Zeb took off his hat and ran his fingers through his hair. It was now about an inch long. "At least when you cut it, you didn't do it with sheep shears," he said. Hannah grinned.

They stopped at Foley's General Store. "I'll meet you back here in about an hour," Zeb said. Hannah nodded as she climbed the steps to the door.

As Zeb headed down Silver Street to Natchez Under-the-Hill, the sun had already burned off most of the early morning fog.

He stopped at a Levee Street building on the river side of the road. A sign hung over the door.

HENRY YADKIN
SAIL MAKER

Zeb entered the sail maker's shop. The morning sun streamed into the big room, and sails and fabric hung from the ceiling in neat rows. Zeb was immediately aware of the not unpleasant musty smell of canvas and hemp rope, and the faint tang of turpentine.

The sail maker, seated at the far end of a table, was pushing a large curved needle up through heavy canvas. He looked up as Zeb's footsteps echoed softly on the wood floor.

Zeb pulled a sheet of paper from his pocket. "Mr. Yadkin?"

The man nodded. "What can I do for you?"

"Do you ever make tents? I'd like a tent somethin' like this, in two pieces like an army tent."

The sail maker looked at the drawing. "A tent about a foot higher and a foot wider than the army-issue tent, with one-foot side walls? It'll take about a week. And I need a deposit."

Zeb nodded. He looked around the room.

"I was surprised Natchez has a sail maker. You can't have many sails to make here."

The man pulled the thread through the canvas. "Most of my sail making is for the keelboats headed downriver to New Orleans. Those boats need sails to help them get upriver, at least back to Natchez."

"And the big sails?"

"We do get a few big ships, oceangoing vessels, coming up from New Orleans. It's usually a difficult journey against that strong current. But this time a' year there's often a strong southerly wind."

Mr. Yadkin paused. I hear they're building a boat that's meant to run on steam. It's supposed to go not only down the Mississippi, but upriver as well!" He shook his head. "I doubt it could make it. But if it did, it sure would change my line of work."

$\sim$

Zeb stopped at the bank, then went by the *Weekly Chronicle*. Inside, a man was kneeling on the floor, picking up pieces of type. He looked up as Zeb came in. Zeb stared down at the man. "You!" he said. "You're the man I saw back at Mt. Locust Inn. Ya told me to look for the bald-headed man!"

The man stood up and squinted at Zeb. "Cut your hair, didn't you?" he said. "Did you find your grampa?"

Zeb nodded. "Yes, thank you. Sir, when we met, you asked me about my uncle Ira. Do you know him?"

"We were roommates at the University of Virginia. Good friends ever since. He's the one who told me that Natchez needed a newspaper."

Zeb kneeled down. "Let me give you a hand with that type."

"So Ira Hamilton put you to work, did he?"

Zeb nodded, gathering the lead letters in his hands. "I was a printer's devil for Uncle Ira, but I'm not lookin' for a job."

"What can I do for you, then?"

Zeb dropped the type gently into a small wooden box. "Grampa wanted a copy of the newspaper, and he wanted me to ask if you had any news from the Nashville or Franklin area."

The editor stood and leafed through papers on his desk. "Nope, nothing from Nashville or Franklin," he said.

"What do you hear about the steamboat bein' built?"

"Pittsburgh paper says it'll leave this month. If it ever reaches Natchez, I plan to be on the dock interviewing everybody."

Zeb left the *Weekly Chronicle* and went back to Mr. Yadkin's shop to leave the tent deposit. Now that the haze had lifted from the river, he could see the reefed sails of a few ships through the window of the sail maker's shop. *Those are the first oceangoing vessels I've ever seen,* he said to himself.

The sail maker put Zeb's golden eagle in a metal box. "That's a British merchant ship," he said, pointing to the tallest one. "I'd stay away from that vessel if I were you. One of the officers and two sailors off that ship came in here this morning to ask about sails, and then they went next door to the ship's chandler and asked for prices of supplies. But they didn't seem to be really interested so much in supplies as they were in seeing the dock area. We saw 'em talking with some of the street kids who hang around the docks, and we both got a bad feelin' about 'em. Don't know what they're up to."

He paused and stared out the open doors toward the docks. "But there *is* a possibility. They could be paying some of the locals to form a press gang."

"What *are* press gangs?"

"Press gangs look for young men like you, young men who are strong and able."

"For what?"

"If a press gang caught you, you'd be declared a deserter from the Royal Navy. You'd spend the rest of your life on board one ship or another."

"A deserter! I could easily prove I was never a British seaman!"

"Who would you prove it to? The people who have pressed you into service?"

Zeb paused. "But why do they do it?"

Yadkin sat back at the table and began sewing again. "Some British seamen *are* deserting. The conditions aboard ship are terrible. Discipline is extremely harsh, and the men haven't been paid in months. The Royal Navy, the most powerful in the world, is suddenly weak for lack of adequate ship's crews."

"So they round up a lot of Kaintucks who don't know a thing about ships?"

"Sure. They're after young men they can train. They also stop our merchant ships on the high seas. They take every able-bodied sailor off those ships, claiming that they're English deserters. Most of the men they press into service are American men with wives and families back here. It's caused a lot of grief."

The sail maker paused. "If you go down to the docks, watch out. You might get far more excitement than you bargained for."

When Zeb left Mr. Yadkin's, he could see the top of the masts of the sailing ship over the roof. In spite of the sail maker's warning, Zeb couldn't resist taking a closer look at the square rigger.

He didn't see any reason to be afraid. The ship was anchored in the deep part of the river, some distance from the floating docks. There appeared to be little activity aboard. Several men struggled with their oars against the river current as they rowed a large boat laden with barrels and boxes to the ship.

I wonder, he thought, *what it'd be like to go to sea, to be a merchant seaman. They must see some wonderful places.*

He wrinkled his nose at the dead fish stink of the docks.

A number of men were standing on the last dock. They seemed to be busy with the boxes and barrels and cloth sacks stacked up for transfer to the ship. Zeb pushed through them and looked over the edge into the well of a boat that was identical to the one being rowed out to the ship. The large rowboat was almost filled, and the crew was about to shove off. The man in charge looked up at him and smiled. "Want to see what a real ship is like? You can go out with us. We'll bring you back after they unload the cargo."

Zeb noticed the smirks on the faces of some of the sailors. He had done enough betting on horse races to know that they knew something he didn't know. As much as he would have liked to see the ship, he decided not to go with them. He shook his head and stepped away from the edge of the dock, backing into one of the men standing there. "Sorry," he said.

Suddenly, two strong arms wrapped around him from behind, pinning Zeb's arms to his sides. "Hey!" Zeb shouted.

"What's going on?" When he was lifted off his feet, he kicked wildly. Another man grabbed his legs and tied them together. He was thrown facedown on the dock. Someone knelt on the middle of his back and tied his hands behind him.

A voice from the boat called to the man kneeling on his back. "Not too ruddy tight, man. If 'e loses a hand, 'e's no use to us. We won't get a farthin' for 'im."

The man slightly loosened the rope around Zeb's wrists.

The voice from the boat said, "We don't want to take any of the gentry, either. They can make it a bit difficult for us. That one isn't dressed like a Kaintuck."

He called up to Zeb. "What's your name, lad? Where're you from?"

Zeb could hardly breathe. "My name," he croaked, "is Zebulon D'Evereux. Let me go!"

The man kneeling on his back roared with laughter. "Zebulon D'Evereux?" he shouted. Zeb sagged. *I know that voice.* The man gave Zeb's side a vicious kick and flipped him over on his back. Zeb looked up into the face of Sergeant Scruggs!

Zeb looked from one side to the other, hoping that some of the other men on the dock would help him. They were all grinning at him. *They're all part of it!*

"I never would've recognized you," the sergeant said. He shouted down to the men in the boat, "You can leave. This one's mine. When I get through with him, he won't be of no use to nobody."

When the sergeant pulled his foot back to kick him again, Zeb rolled out of reach and then kicked at the sergeant's legs with his bound feet. The other men stood by and laughed. The sergeant grinned. "Gonna try to fight me?" He pulled his foot back again.

96

An explosive *crack* made the sergeant jump. He whirled around, grasping the back of his leg. Then he bent his knees, crouched, ready to fight, his face in a ferocious grin.

The only thing that makes a noise like that is a whip, Zeb thought. *But how can Grampa be down here?* Then he heard another familiar voice. "Sergeant! You mess with my partner and you mess with me! You saw how he was ready to fight ya, even tied and bound. That's what a partner of Lonnie Champ is like. We don't never give up."

Zeb rolled on his side. Lonnie Champ stood on the dock coiling a bullwhip. He smiled at Zeb. "I been practicin'. I ain't as good as yer granddad, but I kin teach the sergeant how ta dance."

One of the men who had been helping the sergeant began to move toward Lonnie Champ. The flatboat fighter pointed a finger at the approaching man. "I'm a bear!" he shouted. "I'm a alligator! I'm a cottonmouth snake! See that feather there in my hat? I'm cock o' the walk. No man has ever whupped me, in fair fight or foul, and that includes the sergeant here." He lowered his voice to a menacing growl. "You take one more step and it'll be yer last."

The man stepped back. Lonnie Champ lifted his chin toward Zeb. "You men! Untie my partner, while I deal with the sergeant here."

A couple of men moved toward Zeb.

Lonnie Champ snapped the whip again and the sergeant howled, holding on to his arm this time. Lonnie pointed toward Levee Street. "You best start runnin', Sergeant. Don't worry. I'll be right behind you. I'm gonna teach you how to dance. Gonna do it every time you mess with my partner."

The sergeant sidled past Lonnie Champ, watching the whip. When he saw the whip arm move back, he ran off the dock with Lonnie behind him, snapping the whip at his britches.

One of the men in the boat yelled up to the other members of the gang, "Quick, bring 'im to the edge of the dock and we'll take 'im to the ship."

Zeb heard a noise behind him. He turned his head. It was Mr. Yadkin. "Untie that man," the sail maker ordered in a low, angry voice that demanded to be obeyed.

The man in charge of the boat shouted, "Don't listen to that old man. Just sits around all day, sewing sails."

One of the men on the dock shook his head. "We gotta live here. You don't. Ain't nobody wants to get on the wrong side of Lonnie Champ."

The man in the boat cursed and then ordered the sailors at the oars to get underway. "We best return to the ship and tell the cap'n. He'll probably pull up anchor," he said. "That sail maker'll go for the constable. We'll be out of business."

Zeb could hear the man in the boat giving orders. "Shove off." Then moments later, "On the port side.... *Stroke!* Now all together, *stroke!*" Zeb heard the creak and groan of oars in leather oarlocks as the sailors struggled against the current.

The men on the docks untied Zeb and stepped back, watching Mr. Yadkin. He scowled at the three men. "You can go," he ordered, "but if I see you down at the docks again, I'll notify the constable. Press gangs are illegal in this country. You will be charged with kidnapping."

As the men slipped away into the alleys between the riverfront buildings, Zeb stood up and rubbed his wrists. "Thank you, Mr. Yadkin," he said. "I should've listened to you and stayed away from that ship. I can't believe I was so stupid."

"You were very lucky, young man."

"I know. I can't thank you enough," Zeb said. He looked back at the dock, shaken. "Why isn't the government doing anything about press gangs?"

"You men take one more step and it'll be yer last."

"They say that nothing short of war will stop it. But the U.S. Navy isn't powerful enough to challenge the Royal Navy."

As they turned to walk back to the sail maker's shop, Zeb was suddenly overwhelmed by what might have happened. "Why doesn't the constable arrest the press gangs? Why doesn't he go out to the ship right now and force them to release their captives?"

"The constable and his deputy would have no way to force the captain to give up the men," the sail maker replied. "Look, Zeb, they've already got men in the riggin', gettin' those sails ready to up-anchor and leave this port."

Zeb nodded, then looked up the alley where the press gang had gone. "What about the locals workin' as a press gang? Can't the constable arrest 'em?"

"I'm going now to talk to him. I should've talked to him earlier about my suspicions. But at least now, I know who the British sailors recruited into the press gang. The problem is getting proof. Those men on the docks can claim they were simply innocent bystanders forced to comply with the British. They did untie you...."

"I sure was lucky," Zeb said, "that you and Lonnie Champ came along."

"I'm not so sure it was luck. I got the feeling Lonnie Champ's been watching out for you. He called you his partner, didn't he?"

"I guess we are partners," Zeb said. He thanked Mr. Yadkin again for his help. "Your voice sure sounded different when you told those men to untie me," he said.

"I was bos'n—the officer in charge of the deck hands—in the Continental Navy and later when the U.S. Navy was formed. You don't forget how to talk to sailors."

CHAPTER THIRTEEN

The Closed Carriage

October 26, 1811

Zeb said good-bye to Mr. Yadkin, then went back to where Maggie was tethered and rode the little horse back along Levee Street. When he reached Silver Street, Lonnie Champ was waiting for him. "I don't think the sergeant'll bother ya any more today," he said. "But you better keep an eye out for 'im whenever ya come down here."

Zeb slipped off Maggie and offered his hand. "I want to thank you, Mr. Champ, for your help today."

"Zeb, I meant it when I called you my partner. Yer the only one knows I've got two broken ribs, and you ain't told nobody. But it won't be long 'fore someone'll find out, and then I'll need a partner for sure. I could teach you how to fight—"

"Wouldn't it be best for you to get away from here, until your ribs heal?"

"Where would I go? I ain't got much money. Those men what left me for dead, that mornin' ya found me? They took all I had from bettin' on my fights. Once these ribs heal, I'll head back north on the Nashville Road and pick up another flat-boat. But right now, I jes gotta lie low."

"Mr. Champ...Lonnie," Zeb said. "I've got an idea. I'll be

back in a few days and we can talk about it. You still in that tavern of Dancey Moore's?"

"Yeah. He lets me stay fer free, if I kin keep the peace.... Ain't said nothin' 'bout kickin' me out since I stuck up fer you, neither. Usually jes me lookin' at them what's causin' trouble in Moore's tavern is enough, but if somebody decides to find out if I kin fight, I'm done fer."

"Leave your things with Mr. Yadkin. If what I'm thinkin' about works out, we'll want to leave here without anybody payin' much attention."

Zeb mounted the little horse again and rode up Silver Street toward Foley's in Natchez. As he rounded the corner near Foley's, he was surprised not to see Hannah waiting impatiently for him. But he knew he was a lot later than he had said he would be. He slipped off Maggie and tethered her to the rail. *She must still be inside,* he thought. *It* is *getting a bit chilly out here.*

He went in and looked around the store. She was nowhere in sight. He looked outside and suddenly realized Hannah's horse was no longer tethered to the rail.

Zeb approached Mr. Foley. "Have you seen a girl in here...dressed like a boy, short hair—"

"You asking about Hannah McAllister? She was here for a long time." He pointed to a chair. "Sat over there, waiting for somebody, looking over that book with the fashions and patterns. She had a notebook with her and was writing in it the last time I saw her."

"Where'd she go?"

"A carriageload of women came in, and I lost sight of her. When I looked up again, she was gone."

Zeb ran outside and looked up and down the street. He ran over to the next block and then circled the block around

Foley's. Then he came back into the general store and sat down where Hannah had been sitting. He looked at the fashion book she had left on the floor. A piece of paper was sticking out. He pulled it out of the book. "Zeb" was written in large letters on it. He turned it over.

Something has come up. I am all right. I just need to follow someone. I'll be back as soon as I can.
Hannah

Zeb jumped up and ran to the door, looking up and down the street. Still nothing. All he could do was wait.

He was leafing through the book when she came cantering up to Foley's. He ran outside and was about to shout at her, but she quickly shook her head. It reminded him of how they learned to communicate with no words at all on their trip down the Natchez Road. Neither said anything until Zeb was mounted and they were moving up the street toward home. "I know I must've worried you," Hannah said in a shaky voice, "but I just had to follow them."

"Follow who? Are you all right?"

"I think I might've seen some of the Mason gang—the outlaws I was with."

"Here in Natchez?"

"A fancy closed carriage, black with a family crest on the doors, pulled up in front of Foley's. Five women got out. They were wearing beautiful clothes. The driver of the carriage looked so much like Noah, the head of the Mason gang, that I went over to the window to get a better look. He was all dressed up, but he looked like Noah and he was yelling at those horses like him, too."

"What did you do?"

"I didn't want to get too close, in case they might recognize me. There was one who looked a little like Trudy, but she walked right by and didn't even notice me."

"Maybe you were mistaken."

"Maybe I was. They only had three women with babies and Elizabeth when I was with them. Now there are four women and one that looks like Elizabeth. If it is the outlaws, they must've kidnapped somebody else on the way back. Anyway, when they left, I followed 'em. They drove down a little side street off of Jefferson. I caught up with 'em in time to see the carriage turn into the circular drive of a huge white house."

"A house like that'd cost a fortune and so would a good closed carriage."

"Yeah, but the Mason gang had plenty of money."

"From robbin' Kaintucks?"

"No. From merchants, who had horses and sometimes thousands of dollars in gold coins with 'em. The gang knew that lots of merchants don't trust the banks."

"How'd the outlaws manage to carry that much money?"

"They always buried most of it. Lots of nights I'd hear 'em talk about digging it up and living like rich planters."

Hannah sighed. "I can't be sure it was them," she said. "Let's not tell my mama about it. It'd worry her a lot."

They rode on in silence for a while. Zeb told her about the press gang and Lonnie Champ saving his life again.

After a few moments Zeb said, "I'm gonna ask your parents if Lonnie can stay at your house. That bedroom I'm in has two beds. Maybe he can share it with me. He has a couple of broken ribs and will be in real serious trouble if anyone ever finds out."

"Maybe my father can take a look at those ribs, tell him what to do."

They rode quietly for a while. About halfway to Washington, Zeb spoke.

"Hannah, why are your friends in your class actin' so strange? Are you and Katie leavin' them out?"

Hannah looked surprised. "No. Mama thinks it's just my Choctaw boys' clothes, but I can't tell her the truth. When I invited 'em to come over to the house, one of them said that her mama doesn't want her to visit back and forth like we used to do." Hannah looked up at Zeb, her eyes moist. "I think it's 'cause of what happened to me and 'cause of the color of my skin."

"Oh, Hannah!" Zeb cried out. "People who talk like that are stupid! Do you know what Grampa says when someone talks like that? 'If you've got three horses just alike, except that one is white, one is black, and one is bay, which one is the best?' The other man will always say, 'The color of the horse don't make no difference.' 'Exactly,' my grampa says."

They rode the rest of the way home in silence. Zeb had to keep reminding himself to look like a tired man on a sad little cob. Dancey Moore and his horse wranglers would still be looking for a tall, shaggy-haired boy on a big, proud horse.

～

About a week later, Mr. Culpepper and Katie were seated at the breakfast table when Zeb walked in. Mr. Culpepper looked up. "Mornin', Zeb. What are your plans for today?"

Zeb sat down at the table. Everything smelled like home. "May I borrow Maggie again?" he asked. "I'd like to ride her and lead Kapucha into Natchez. I hafta pick up the tent, the new clothes I had made, and some supplies for the trip."

Mr. Culpepper poured some coffee in his cup. "Why don't you take the wagon?" he said. "You can manage two horses, can't you?"

"Oh, yes, sir. The wagon would be fine. I'll use our new draft horses. It'll give me a chance to get to know them."

Katie interrupted. "If Zeb is going into Natchez today with the wagon, may I go with him? The shoemaker should have my boots ready by now."

"That's fine with me if it's all right with you, Zeb."

"No problem at all," Zeb said. "Hannah and Mrs. McAllister are plannin' to ride in with me. I'm sure they'll find the wagon more comfortable."

"Hannah's going in again?" Katie asked.

"Her mama wants the two of them to pick out all the fabric for her dresses so the seamstress can get started."

Zeb hitched up two of his grampa's new draft horses to the big wagon. Mr. Culpepper helped him put some heavy planks across to serve as seats.

Zeb and Katie climbed up on the front bench and drove to the McAllister house. When he stopped for Hannah and her mother, Katie moved back to sit with Hannah. Zeb told them proudly that since the McAllisters had agreed to let Lonnie Champ, his partner, stay at their house, he might be picking up Lonnie today. He hadn't told anyone but Hannah and his grandfather about the press gang. He planned to talk with Captain Morrison whenever he reappeared at the Culpepper farm.

Zeb busied himself with the pleasure of getting to know the beautiful big draft horses. Behind him, he could hear the murmur of voices and the occasional laughter.

"Can you imagine me in dresses, Katie?" Hannah asked. "Dresses down to my ankles, ankle shoes with bows, straw hats: one for weekdays and one for Sunday." She mimicked Miss Phillipa's voice. "'The Sunday hat will have a ribbon around the crown which will fall gracefully down your back.'" The two girls collapsed with laughter.

He smiled. *How wonderful it is,* he thought, *that Hannah is able to laugh. It's almost as if she's forgotten the Mason gang and what they did to her....*

He left the three of them at Foley's. "I'll see you right here in about two hours!" he shouted over his shoulder as he drove the team away.

When he got to the sail maker's shop, Mr. Yadkin had the tent ready, coated with beeswax and turpentine. It was now the color of butternuts. He and Mr. Yadkin unfolded and set it up outside, each one holding a tent pole. The strong odor of turpentine burned his eyes and his nose. "How do you stand it?" Zeb croaked.

"You get used to it. That stink'll be gone in a couple of months, maybe sooner, if you leave it out day and night, rain or shine."

Zeb looked at the tent and smiled. It was just what he wanted. He paid Mr. Yadkin the balance of the bill and loaded the tent, folded once again, up into the back of the wagon. He turned to shake Mr. Yadkin's hand.

"Just a minute, Zeb," the sail maker said. "Lonnie Champ tells me that you may have something for him."

"I do. I need to find a way to contact him. Dr. McAllister has agreed to let Mr. Champ stay at the McAllister place for now. Then he can go back up the trail with us to wherever he came from."

Mr. Yadkin smiled. "You really have become his partner, haven't you? He doesn't want you to go near the tavern. Dancey Moore has his men out looking for you."

Mr. Yadkin called over one of the street boys and gave him a message for Lonnie Champ. The boy returned in minutes with Champ by his side, and the sail maker gave the boy a coin.

"It'd be best if you left for Natchez as soon as possible, Zeb," Yadkin said. "And I've got one last thing for you." He went back into the shop and reappeared with a small shovel. "This is a Spanish army shovel. I've had it a long time, but I doubt I'll ever use it. I want you to have it for your trip north. You'll need it to make a trench around your new tent."

"Thank you, sir. I really appreciate it."

Lonnie Champ climbed up in the wagon and sat with Zeb on the driver's bench. Zeb told him all about the arrangements he had made with Dr. McAllister. He turned the team onto the street and clucked them into a slow trot back up Silver Street.

Zeb loved the feeling of controlling so much power. *These animals are so strong. Just a gentle movement of the reins and they do whatever I want.*

Lonnie Champ grinned at him. "You really enjoy drivin' this team, dontcha?"

Zeb just grinned in reply.

A beautiful closed carriage passed Zeb and Lonnie going the opposite direction, and Zeb noted that each of the doors had glass windows. The carriage wood was dark with a light-colored inlay on the door, like a family crest.

Lonnie Champ dipped his head as if there were royalty inside the carriage. "Dancey Moore says that they's only two fine carriages in Natchez, and that's one of 'em. They was left here by the Spanish, and everybody wants one of 'em."

The white man driving the carriage snaked a long whip out and the pair of horses picked up their gait. They were big horses, more suitable for pulling heavy loads or a plow, in Zeb's opinion.

Zeb frowned, thinking. But in a moment he and Lonnie were at Foley's, and Zeb pulled the horses up in front. He smiled down at Mrs. McAllister and the girls. "This is my partner,

Lonnie Champ. He's the one who saved me from the sergeant. He's the person I've been tellin' you about."

No one responded. Katie Culpepper climbed up into the wagon without saying a word to Zeb. Hannah's mother was next, her mouth set in a grim, straight line.

Hannah climbed up last. She watched the fancy carriage as it rounded the corner at the far end of the street, and when she turned back to look up at Zeb, her face was pale.

As Zeb drove, he could hear no more than a low, angry murmur from the passengers behind him. It was nothing like the laughter and high spirits on the way into town. What's the matter? he wondered. *Are they mad I picked up Lonnie? He must feel like he's not wanted.*

Finally, Hannah's mother raised her voice. "Hannah, I insist you tell me what happened. Why are you so frightened?"

Zeb halted the horses and looked over his shoulder. Hannah sat with her head down, her hands wrapped tightly around her knees. "I can't talk about it," she whispered.

Her mother took her by the shoulders. "Hannah," she said angrily. "Something has frightened you. You must tell me what happened in there."

"It was Elizabeth!" Hannah blurted out. "That woman with all the fancy clothes, with the closed carriage and the driver! That was Elizabeth, one of the women in the Mason gang." She sobbed.

Hannah's mother shook her head. "Are you sure?"

"I'm sure," Hannah said, wiping her hand across her eyes. "When you were talking to Mr. Foley, I wandered over to the other side of the store...."

She ran her fingers through her hair. "She was over there. When I realized who she was, I turned to run. She grabbed my arm and yanked me close to her."

"She grabbed my arm and yanked me close to her."

"What did she say?"

"She said…she said if I ever told anybody who she was, the gang would find me and skin me alive!"

Hannah looked up at her mother. "Mama," she said, "she can find us. She said there aren't likely to be many McAllisters in Washington."

"I can't believe those outlaws are here in Natchez, threatening you!" Hannah's mother turned to Zeb. "Turn around! Turn around now! We've got to go see the constable. Hurry!"

"Oh, Mama! Please don't do anything! If the constable starts looking for 'em, they'll know I told, and they'll surely come and find me. That man driving the carriage was Noah, the head of the gang. Elizabeth is mean, but the men are much worse."

Hannah's mother pulled her close. "Oh, Hannah. I had hoped that was all behind you, that you would be able to forget…."

Hannah shook her head. "I'll never forget."

Lonnie Champ slid closer to Zeb and said in a low voice, "You keep your eyes on the road in front of us. I'll watch the back." He climbed from the driver's bench and sat next to Katie.

"Mama, I'm so afraid!" Hannah cried, and her mother hugged her tighter. "Why did they hafta come here?"

"I wonder where she got that carriage and those fine clothes," Katie said.

"They had a lot of money stored all along the trail."

Mrs. McAllister pulled Hannah against her and rocked her. "And now they're in Natchez with all that money," she said. "And they've got to find a way to keep you quiet."

Lonnie leaned forward. "If I kin help in any way, ma'am…."

"You can," she said. "Now that you'll be staying with us, you'll be able to give Hannah a little more protection. Zeb can't be with her all the time."

"I'll look out fer her, Mrs. McAllister. You kin count on it."

CHAPTER FOURTEEN

Hannah

November 28, 1811

I t was late November when Captain Morrison and the Mounted Light Dragoon patrol moved onto the back forty acres of the Culpepper farm. There were eleven of them in all: Captain Morrison, Sergeant Douglas, and nine men.

The men put up tents in a neat row alongside the stream running through the back of the property. They dug a deep hole a good distance downstream from the campsite, for a privy. They dug a shallow hole for the cooking pit in the center of the camp, and they designated an upstream part of the creek for drinking water and a downstream part for bathing and washing clothes.

Captain Morrison's tent looked a lot like Zeb's: about four feet high at the peak, the roof sloping outward toward two one-foot sidewalls. Almost a month had passed since Zeb had brought his tent back to the Culpepper farm, and the turpentine odor had already faded away. He practiced taking it down and putting it up over and over again. It usually took two men to put up a tent quickly, but he couldn't count on his grampa's being able to help him. He wanted to be able to do it himself, and he didn't want to look like a complete fool in front of the dragoons.

~

One afternoon a few days later, Zeb was in the corral working with Kapucha. Since he had loaned Christmas to Lonnie Champ so he would have a big horse to ride, Zeb had worked with Kapucha every day, getting him to accept the bit and to respond to leg signals. The dark gray horse was smart and willing. He was as stocky as Christmas but almost two hands shorter.

Zeb looked up to see Hannah and Dr. McAllister turning off the road and into the stable yard. *Dr. McAllister looks much more alive lately than he did when I first met him,* Zeb thought.

Lonnie Champ followed them on Christmas, a coiled bull-whip hanging from a strap on one side of the saddle. He kept looking from one side of the road to the other, up the road, and then behind him. Even when they were on the Culpepper property, Lonnie Champ didn't relax his vigil. He stayed at the gate to the Culpepper carriageway.

He's taking the job of looking after Hannah very seriously, Zeb thought. *But what could happen to her here?* He sighed. *It wasn't so long ago that I was protecting her—and she was protecting me.*

Hannah was riding one of the horses Mr. Culpepper had loaned her. She rode Suba only in the Culpepper pastures.

"Morning," Zeb said as Dr. McAllister and Hannah approached. "You haven't been ridin' over here with me for a couple of days, Hannah. You all right?"

"I'll tell you all about it," she said quietly.

"Morning, Zeb. Ah, good, there's your grandfather," Dr. McAllister said, waving to Zeb's grampa on the porch.

"He's been walkin' around a lot, tryin' to get some exercise," Zeb said. "But he's sure gettin' impatient to take his arm out of that sling."

Dr. McAllister turned back to Zeb. "I'll go take care of that now. Then I want to see the captain."

Dr. McAllister turned to Hannah. "You may tell Zeb and Katie about our decision. I'll be a while." He dismounted, tethered his horse, and crossed the stable yard to the porch.

Hannah and Zeb dismounted and led the horses to the barn.

"We're all going back to Yowani." Hannah sighed, looking down at her boots.

"Really? Hannah, that's great news! We'll be traveling together at least that far."

"It isn't all great news, Zeb. I love Yowani, but I love it here, too. I love being with Katie on this farm and being able to see Natchez when I feel like it. But I hafta go. It isn't safe for me here now."

"What made you change your mind?"

"We've told Captain Morrison about the outlaws and where they live," she said. "He told Mama that unless we go back to Yowani, if there's even one of the gang members free, I'll be in danger. I'm the only one who can identify 'em."

"What'll the captain do?"

"He's waiting until he's sure that they're all in Natchez to arrest 'em."

That afternoon Captain Morrison, accompanied by Sergeant Douglas, rode up over the hill from the dragoon encampment and down into the farmyard. He had asked Hannah and her parents, Zeb and his grampa, Katie and Mr. Culpepper, and Walter to meet with him there. He was going to let them know how he planned to deal with the outlaw gang.

"I want to thank you, Walter," Captain Morrison said, "for all your help. It really paid off to have you talk with servants to find out if the outlaws had other houses in Natchez. We'll be watching each one."

He turned to the group. "We'll strike tomorrow night. The place will be surrounded. "

"Oh, sir!" Hannah cried. "Don't forget, three babies are with 'em."

"I know. That's what is going to make this difficult."

~

Everyone was edgy, but they tried to busy themselves with chores. At about four in the afternoon, the dragoon patrol headed toward Natchez: ten men double file, with Captain Morrison in the lead. They wore full battle dress.

It was well after the evening meal when they returned. The men were grim-faced, stern, and angry-looking. Captain Morrison kept slapping his quirt against his leg.

Captain Morrison told the sergeant to take the men back to the encampment. He asked the Culpeppers, McAllisters, Zeb and his grampa, and Walter to come up onto the back porch of the farmhouse.

When they were settled he said, "I'm afraid that we were outwitted."

"Oh, no!" Hannah cried. "They got away?"

"We were able to arrest four women and six men. But when we got there, Elizabeth and Noah were long gone."

Hannah sagged against her mother. "Oh, Mama! Elizabeth is terrible. She…" Hannah looked at the pain in her mother's face. "Never mind," she said. "I don't want to talk about it."

"What happened, Captain Morrison?" Cracker Ryan asked.

"It is clear from a search of the houses that the gang had been planning to leave for some time. They probably decided to go as soon as they saw Hannah, because they knew she could identify them."

"So?..." Zeb's grampa started.

"The two who got away had double-crossed the other outlaws, too. We found a large pile of lead shot and rifle balls in a corner of a shed."

"They were heavily armed?" Zeb asked.

"No. We think they emptied the shot boxes and used them to carry the fortune in gold coins they had stolen. Filled with gold coins, each box would probably weigh about the same as a box of lead shot. They must have moved those boxes of gold down to the docks long before we got there and arranged with a boat to take the two of them to New Orleans."

"How do you know all of this?" Cracker Ryan asked.

"The men we caught told us. They are furious. They know they were left to be arrested so Elizabeth and Noah could have all the money."

Captain Morrison turned to Hannah. "We plan to grant these women immunity if they testify against the men. We have no real way of proving where the money came from."

"Those women didn't travel with the gang voluntarily, Captain," Hannah said, "except Elizabeth. The other three were taken by force the way I was. Two of 'em tried to run away, but their babies' crying gave them away in the woods. They were easy to find, and Elizabeth whipped 'em somethin' awful."

Hannah took a deep breath and continued. "Trudy, the youngest one, ran away when we got near her hometown. She took some of the gold and just disappeared. But the outlaws didn't seem to be worried. We just camped there in the woods for about ten days. One day she rode back into the camp with a horse and a donkey loaded down with packages: food and clothes and gunpowder and shot. She said she just went to get some provisions. She told the women later that when she got home, her family wouldn't take her in. She had no place to go, so she came back.

"Noah said it was a lesson to all of us. 'If you run away,' he said, 'your families won't take you back, and you'll probably die in the forest.' After that, no one tried to leave."

She turned to Zeb. "Now you know why I was so scared when we stood in my backyard waiting for someone to come to the door."

CHAPTER FIFTEEN

Lonnie Champ

December 2, 1811

The next morning, as Hannah and Mrs. McAllister prepared to ride to the Culpepper horse farm, Zeb sat on Kapucha in the street in front of their house, and Lonnie was mounted on Christmas, ready to follow. Captain Morrison had told them that he was sure Elizabeth and Noah had left for New Orleans, but it was always wise to be prepared.

Lonnie Champ had taken to copying Zeb's grampa in every way he could.

He carried the coiled bullwhip hitched to the saddle exactly as Zeb's grampa did. He often snapped the whip at leaves on trees or anything else that provided a target. Zeb smiled to himself. *He probably wants to be known as "Cracker Champ." But he's gonna have quite a surprise if he tries that near any horse other than Christmas. Most horses will shy at that noise.*

They turned into the Culpepper driveway. Hannah's mother dismounted and climbed the stairs. She and Mrs. Lodge sat on the porch, sewing and watching. Katie was waiting for Hannah. "C'mon," she said, running toward the barn. "We have six horses to exercise this morning."

Cracker Ryan was already in the corral with Mary and Beth Lodge. Mary was mounted on one of the smaller of the saddle horses, trotting around. She gave the horse a little kick and he moved from a trot to a canter. Cracker Ryan held up his hand. "Not yet, Mary," he said with a smile. "I'll tell you when you can do that. Let me get Beth going first."

Zeb's grampa helped put Beth up on a pony. By the time they had made the complete circle, she had her hands off the pommel. She gestured and called to Mary with a timid, "Look at me."

Zeb slipped off Kapucha, tethered him to the rail, and entered the corral. Cracker Ryan handed him the reins. Whenever they worked with young children learning to ride, his grampa would get them started and then, when they showed less fear, Zeb would take over.

Mr. Culpepper rode up to the corral and pulled his horse next to Lonnie's. "Cracker," he said, "would you like to ride fences with me this morning? One of those fool colts got out of the second pasture...." Suddenly he turned in his saddle, shading his eyes with his hand.

Zeb climbed the rail and looked toward the carriageway as five men galloped their horses into the stable yard and pulled up in front of the barn. A cloud of dust stretching from the road to the barn made it impossible to see who they were. He could just make out Walter, the stable hand, who stood in front of the barn door with a pitchfork in his hands.

"Oh, no. Something's wrong!" Mr. Culpepper shouted. He and Lonnie Champ galloped over to where Walter was standing. Zeb lifted Beth off the pony. His grampa called Mary to him and helped her dismount. "You girls run up to the porch."

Mary protested, "But Mr. Ryan, you said—"

"First thing about learning to ride is following orders. Now get up on that porch. We'll get back to ridin' later."

Cracker Ryan grabbed his whip, and then he and Zeb ran across the paddock to stand on either side of Walter.

Zeb could see that each of the men who had just ridden into the yard was carrying a pistol in his hand.

He glanced up at the back porch. Hannah's mother and Mrs. Lodge were hurrying the two little girls into the house.

Mr. Culpepper stared at Dancey Moore.

Moore grinned at him. "You know why I'm here," he said. "Yer hidin' a racehorse that belongs to me. I want that horse now." He looked toward the barn. "And I may just take one more for all the trouble you've caused me. We'll look 'em over and decide if you have any worth takin'."

Lonnie Champ began to move Christmas toward Dancey Moore. Moore cocked the pistol and pointed it at him. "Didn't recognize you at first, Champ. I wondered what had happened to you. So this is where you've gone, and after all I've done for you."

Lonnie kept moving toward him. Moore shook his head. "Don't make me use this," he said.

He turned in his saddle and lifted his chin at Zeb and his grampa. "I'm glad to see you two here. That means that my other horse is hidden here as well."

He shook his head. "A couple of worn-out horse breeders, a Negro freeman with only a pitchfork, a scrawny Kaintuck, and a has-been cock of the walk. You think yer gonna stop us from taking those horses? We're armed, and we won't hesitate to use these pistols if we hafta. Now get out of the way."

He pointed to one of his men. "Get down and open that door."

Just then Hannah cantered Suba through the tall grass up to the fence that separated the pasture from the barnyard. The big black mare pranced around a bit, but Hannah had her in control.

Mr. Moore's eyes narrowed at the sight of the horse. "So you admit it," he shouted. "You do have my racehorse! Bring it here!"

Hannah turned and cantered the horse in a large circle, showing off its beautiful stride. Dancey Moore moved his horse over to the fence. "Get off the horse, boy!" he shouted to her. "I'm takin' that one home with me."

Hannah cantered it around once more, as if she didn't hear him.

Moore shouted. "When I give you an order, boy, you do what yer told! Now, get off that horse!"

Hannah shrugged. She pulled Suba in at the far side of the circle and slipped off, then walked slowly toward Mr. Moore, leading the big black horse. When she got about six feet from the fence, she held the reins out for him to take. Dancey Moore sighed with exasperation. "Don't you know nothin', boy?" he said. "You want me to come over there and get that horse myself? You'll never work for me." He dismounted and climbed over the fence. He snatched the reins from her and stroked the horse's long neck.

The stirrups were set for Hannah's legs. As he lowered the stirrup on the left side, he called across the horse to Hannah. "Boy? Lower the stirrup on that side."

Hannah adjusted the stirrups, then the saddle pad.

"Gimme those reins," he growled, grabbing them from her.

Suba, reacting to the sound of his angry voice, kept moving away from him. Moore yanked hard on the reins.

Hannah climbed the fence and stood between Zeb and his grampa. Zeb whispered to her. "What's goin' on, Hannah? Where's Katie?"

"We just needed to hold 'em here a little while longer, Zeb. You'll see."

Moore mounted the horse, trotted Suba in a circle, and then sat deep in the saddle and began to canter the horse. Suba suddenly bucked and twisted. Moore was thrown to the ground. Suba bucked some more, then turned and galloped across the pasture, disappearing behind the hill.

Dancey Moore stood up, slammed his hat against his pants, and put it back on his head. He climbed through the fence and remounted the horse he'd ridden to the farm. He turned the horse and shouted at Culpepper. "I'm still gonna take that horse. I bought her and she's mine! When I get through with her, she won't behave like that."

Dancey Moore sneered at Culpepper. "I've got five men, each with a loaded pistol." He nodded to the men. They pulled the hammers back on the pistols. "I should say, each with a *cocked*, loaded pistol. And some of us have an extra pistol, just in case. There are five of you. One pistol ball for each. Now, Culpepper, go get that black racehorse and that saddle horse I bought. Go get 'em now!" he shouted. "Or we start shooting."

He pointed his gun at the porch. "We saw those women and children up there. We'll take care of them, too, if we hafta. Can't have no witnesses."

While Moore threatened Mr. Culpepper, Lonnie Champ eased the coiled whip into his hand. Zeb tensed. *If he tries to use that whip against these men, we're all dead.*

At that moment, Captain Morrison and the sergeant galloped over the hill with four of the dragoons behind them. The captain held his saber high in front of him.

Dancey Moore's men turned their horses, preparing to run. But two of the dragoons were galloping toward them down the Culpepper driveway. There was no escape.

Zeb ran and opened the pasture gate. The captain and his men trotted through and then slowed the horses to a walk. The six men split into two groups of three, taking positions on either side of Dancey Moore and his men. Their faces were stern and unforgiving.

Each man pulled his dragoon pistol out of its holster, cocked it, and pointed it at Moore and his men.

The four men behind Dancey Moore put their hands in the air, still holding their pistols. Moore pulled his horse back a step.

The captain slammed the saber back into its scabbard. "Dancey Moore!" he said loudly. "First, you will uncock that pistol. Then, holding it by the barrel, you will hand it to one of my men."

He lifted his head and looked at the four men behind Moore. They still had their hands in the air. "You men may lower your hands. Hold your pistols by the barrel and hand them to my men. If you have more than one, tell them now or suffer the consequences."

Three of the six dragoons walked their horses alongside Dancey Moore's men and relieved them of their weapons. Two of the men pulled an extra pistol out of their belts.

As one of the dragoons took Dancey Moore's pistol, Moore growled at the captain. "Where'd you come from? You got no jurisdiction here. Give me back my gun."

The captain waited until his men had resumed their positions. "I'll ask the questions," he said. "What are *you* doing here?"

Dancey Moore started to talk as if he were trading horses. "Look, Captain," he said, trying to sound reasonable and honest, "I can see why you might misunderstand what's goin' on here, with me and my men holdin' pistols on these rascals. What you don't know is that this boy and his grampa, old man Ryan," he said, pointing at them, "stole two horses that belong to me. They've been hidin' 'em here at Culpepper's farm. We knew they weren't goin' to give 'em back without a fight, so we came prepared."

"Which horses are you talking about?"

"One is a racehorse. I call her Blackie. I paid a thousand dollars for that horse, fair and square."

*Each man pulled his dragoon pistol out of its
holster and cocked it.*

"That horse's name is Suba," Captain Morrison corrected him. "It is registered to Dr. McAllister's daughter, Hannah. You bought that horse from ex-sergeant Michael Scruggs. And you paid him five hundred dollars for it, not a thousand. You knew that he had stolen the horse."

"You can't prove that!"

"I can. The ex-sergeant and I have had a heart-to-heart talk. He owed the United States Army for the price of a horse he lost gambling and a saddle he left somewhere in the forest. We had a warrant for his arrest."

Dancey Moore shrugged as if all that had nothing to do with him.

"When we caught up with him," the captain continued, "he paid what he owed, and I agreed not to take him back to the fort to serve time. But when I saw how much money he had with him, I insisted that he tell me where he got it. He told me all about your arrangement with him."

"Don't make no difference! Ain't my business where he got her. My word against his. It's *my* horse, and I plan to get it back!"

"The constable doesn't see it that way. You and Sergeant Scruggs swore out a false accusation for kidnapping. You made an agreement with the sergeant to steal the horse, and you paid him for it. We have witnesses to all of it."

"There ain't no witnesses. Yer just bluffing. And I bought the other horse fair and square, and I can prove it. Got papers for him."

"The 'other horse'?"

"I bought him from Tate McPhee, saddle, bridle, and all. I paid him top dollar. He told me that old man Ryan was dead, shot by outlaws. The old fool ain't dead, and now he wants his horse back." His voice became louder and more belligerent. "He and that boy stole both horses from me, and I want 'em back!"

"You seem to know a lot about the law."

"I do when it comes to horses. Been dealin' with 'em for almost twenty years."

"You may want to see the magistrate about these two horses. Do it all legally instead of using pistols."

Dancey Moore nodded as if that would be a better way to go about it.

"The magistrate," the captain continued, "may remind you that the penalty for knowingly receiving stolen goods is often as severe as the theft of the goods. You do know what the penalty is for stealing a horse, don't you?" Captain Morrison nodded at his men. "I've seen and heard enough. Dancey Moore...."

Dancey Moore's horse started acting up. Moore had his hands free from the reins, but the horse kept sidling around. Zeb could see that he was pressing one leg and then the other against the horse's flanks. Moore had moved his horse so that it was now between Zeb and his grampa. Moore grabbed the reins and made as if to back up, but he put his hand inside his shirt and pulled out a little pistol. He pointed it at Cracker Ryan's head. "You ain't gonna take me!" he shouted. "Anyone makes a move and this old man is dead!"

He leaned down and said to Zeb's grampa, "Drop that silly whip, old man. Drop it now!"

Cracker Ryan dropped the whip to the ground.

"Don't move," Dancey Moore growled. "I want all of you to get away from here and let me and my men go. Otherwise the famous Cracker Ryan is dead!"

Crack! The little pistol flew out of Moore's hand and fell to the ground. Moore screamed in pain, grasping his hand.

The soldiers quickly moved alongside Dancey Moore and pulled him off his horse. Zeb's grampa was holding his hand over his ear. Lonnie began to coil his whip.

Zeb shouted at Lonnie, "That was a stupid chance you took. That pistol could've fired!"

Lonnie Champ slipped off Christmas. "He hadn't cocked it yet, Zeb," he said quietly. "When I saw 'im begin ta pull the hammer down, I jes knew I had ta move."

Lonnie walked over to Zeb's grampa. "You all right, Mr. Ryan? Did I get yer ear?"

The old man smiled. "No, you didn't. The snap was so loud and so close to my ear, it's still ringing. But no harm done." He looked up at Lonnie Champ. "Nice work."

"Tie each man's hands behind his back while still mounted," Captain Morrison ordered. "Search Dancey Moore thoroughly. Check his boots, too. Then put him on his horse and tie his hands as well. Sergeant Douglas, take three men to escort these horse thieves into Fort Dearborn. We'll hold them with a federal charge of trespassing on army property until we are able to notify the constable."

"Army property!" shouted Dancey Moore.

"That's right!" said Captain Morrison. "While we are camped here, this is army property. You are trespassing!"

The sergeant ordered Dancey Moore to mount and put his hands behind his back. "Wait!" Dancey Moore shouted. "That horse is a stallion. No way I can manage him without control of the reins. You all have guns on me. I ain't gonna run."

Captain Morrison nodded, and the men tied Dancey Moore's hands in front of him. The horse was restless, fidgeting from all the noise and tension while they tied Moore's hands. When the soldiers stepped back, Moore sat without touching the reins. The horse seemed calm and manageable.

Moore glared down at Hannah, "You!" he snarled. "Yeah, you, boy. I know what you done. You put burrs under the back of the saddle of that mare, didn't you? Dancey Moore don't forgive and forget."

Suddenly the horse began to act up again. Dancey Moore had his tied hands up in front of his chest, as if he were praying. The horse started to spin, turning around and around.

Zeb could see Moore's legs, urging the horse on. *What is he up to? If he makes a run for it, they'll surely shoot him. He must know that.*

The horse stopped turning. Moore appeared to have him in control again. *Oh, my God. No!* He screamed, "Move, Hannah! Move!"

As the horse kicked, Lonnie Champ threw himself between Hannah and the stallion's hind legs, shoving Hannah out of the way. The horse kicked Lonnie squarely in the chest. He collapsed to the ground, gasping for breath.

Captain Morrison shouted to the sergeant, "Move all the men to the highway and wait for me there. Take Dancey Moore off that horse! He will walk to Fort Dearborn."

Then he said, "Zeb, go get Dr. McAllister. Bring him back here right away."

Hannah was kneeling on the ground next to Lonnie Champ. Her mother hurried down the porch steps and knelt on his other side. Hannah cried, "Oh, Lonnie, don't die."

Lonnie opened his eyes and looked up at her. "I've had a lot worse than this," he gasped. "But I'm a bear," he whispered. "I'm a alligator, I'm a panther. I'm a cottonmouth. Ain't no man can whup me, fair fight or foul, and don't you forget it." He coughed and winced. Then he put his hand on his chest, grimacing. His eyes closed once again. He sighed. The hand slid slowly to the ground. His face relaxed. Lonnie Champ was dead.

Hannah lifted his head and put it in her lap. She leaned over him and sobbed.

Final Arrangements

December 2, 1811

Lonnie Champ was buried in the Culpepper cemetery. The McAllisters, Zeb and his grampa, Mr. Culpepper and Katie, the Lodge family, and the dragoon patrol in dress uniforms attended. Reverend Lodge conducted the simple ceremony.

"I don't know," he said, "what Lonnie Champ's religious beliefs were. But I do know that he had a fierce loyalty and a good heart. He was a truly good man, and a brave one too."

The soldiers stood at attention, with their rifles by their sides. At the sergeant's nod, they raised their rifles and fired into the air. The funeral was over.

~

On December 7, Captain Morrison assembled all those who were going with the patrol and informed them that he now had his orders. They would be leaving in four days. "You must be ready to leave that morning before sunup," he said, "or be left behind."

He was starting to return to the army encampment when two horsemen rode up the long Culpepper driveway. Each man was leading a heavily laden packhorse. Captain Morrison turned his horse and waited for them. They nodded to each other. "Gentlemen," Captain Morrison said. "Captain," they said.

Captain Morrison turned his horse once again and rode just ahead of the two men back to where the group was still assembled, talking and making plans.

"Let me introduce you," he said to the group, "to the others who will be traveling with us on the Nashville Road. This is Mr. Ebersole and this is Mr. Swanson, both from Pittsburgh. They brought four flatboats down the river and—"

"What we brought down the river is none of anyone's business," Mr. Ebersole said. "I am not interested in making any social contact with these people. Your job, Captain Morrison, is to get us safely to Nashville, nothing else."

"My job," Captain Morrison said, "is to travel from here to Nashville under army orders. Civilians are permitted to go with us, under our protection, at my discretion."

Ebersole looked around the stable yard and the fenced pasture. "At your insistence, we have given up our rooms at the hotel to camp here. Show us where we may put up our tents."

Captain Morrison sat silently upon his horse for a moment, then said, "I will lead you there in just one moment. I want to remind you that I also insisted you exercise these four animals every day. They need to be in good physical condition to handle the strenuous trip north."

"Our horses are in excellent condition."

"Let me remind you once again: If anyone has to stop for any reason, the patrol cannot wait for you. Those are my orders."

Turning his horse, he called over his shoulder, "Follow me."

Everyone began to talk again, excited about the prospect of starting north. Mr. Culpepper said he had something he wanted to discuss with Hannah and Zeb, alone. They walked toward the big barn as they talked. "I know that you want to bring Suba with you on this trip north, Hannah—"

"I do. I can't bear to leave her here. Dancey Moore is gonna get her. I know it."

"I doubt that Dancey Moore will ever be a problem again. But I have an idea that may change your mind about leaving her here."

"What are you thinking about?"

"Ever since I heard that Zeb had raced Suba down in Natchez Under-The-Hill, and that she had won against Perfect Chance—"

"Perfect Chance?" Zeb asked.

"That was the name of the racehorse Suba beat. He's not the best in Natchez, but he often places or shows. He's certainly faster than any of the fillies at the Natchez racetrack."

"But that was just one time," Hannah said.

"That's true, but I've been timing Suba when you and Katie have been racing Suba against Christmas. Her speed is impressive."

"You think we should race her?"

"I think she could be trained and made ready for the spring races. I think she'll do very well, Hannah."

"But if she stays here, I'll miss her terribly."

"I know you will, Hannah. But if you ever had thoughts about racing her, now is the time to do it."

"I'll have to talk with my parents."

"I've already talked with them about it, Hannah. They said it was completely up to you."

"And you think it's a good idea...."

"I do. And if she is as good as I think she is, a foal out of Suba would be a very valuable foal indeed."

Hannah took a long breath, looking out over the pasture at the horses grazing in the far corner. "I'll leave her with you and Katie then, Mr. Culpepper." She sighed. "I wonder if I'll ever be able to watch her race."

Suddenly she stopped. "But what about Dancey Moore? What if he ever gets out of that army prison?"

"I'm sure," Mr. Culpepper said, "that we never need to worry about Dancey Moore again. I know they're guarding him very well. What's more, if I'm right about Suba, she'll be so well-known that stealing her would be impossible. No one could get away with it."

Tears welled up in Hannah's eyes, and she got up and headed for the house. "I'm gonna tell Mama what we've decided."

Zeb rode out to the corral on Kapucha where his grampa was working with the little girls. He and his grampa stood together as the children rode around the ring. Mary was trotting her horse and little Beth was walking the pony, her hands gripping the reins tightly. She looked at Zeb's grampa for approval whenever she passed him.

Zeb was pleased to have an opportunity to talk with his grampa. He told him about the decision to let Culpepper race Suba. Then he told his grampa about an idea he'd been working out involving the draft horses and the missionaries. He spoke with excitement, motioning toward the Lodges, to the McAllisters, and back to himself again. When Zeb was finished, Cracker Ryan clapped him on the back.

"Good thinking, Zeb," Cracker Ryan said, smiling. "That's an excellent plan."

CHAPTER SEVENTEEN

The Road North

December 11, 1811

At last the convoy was lined up and ready to leave. A fine drizzle greeted the column. Mounted on Kapucha, Zeb rode up to the Lodge wagon and offered the family his new, large tent. He and his grampa would use their old tent, which still worked fine, and the Lodges would have shelter as well. He then showed them how to use the two halves of the tent as ponchos as they rode. In a few moments, Mr. and Mrs. Lodge sat on the wagon bench with one of the halves wrapped around them. The other half covered the two girls and the Lodge family possessions in the bed of the wagon.

Captain Morrison rode back to the rear of the convoy, dismounting at the missionaries' wagon to check a wheel. He looked at the rest of the wagon and shook his head. Sarah's husband, Ben, had repaired the old wagon for the time being, but no one expected it to hold for very long. Captain Morrison mounted again and rode to the three dragoons of the rear guard, spoke with them briefly, then cantered back to the head of the convoy.

Zeb and Hannah looked at each other and, without saying a word, moved out of the convoy to the little Culpepper cemetery.

Hannah slipped off Christmas and stood by Lonnie's grave. "Good-bye, Lonnie," she said. "Thank you."

Zeb helped her back up on Christmas and the two rejoined the convoy.

Captain Morrison spoke to Sergeant Douglas, who raised his arm and shouted, "Move out!"

The sergeant and the three dragoons in the lead moved forward immediately, with Captain Morrison and Cracker Ryan just behind them. Following them were Mr. Ebersole and Mr. Swanson, each man leading a draft horse loaded with pack baskets. Next in line rode Hannah on Christmas, then three dragoons, and last were Hannah's mother on one draft horse and Dr. McAllister on another.

Following them were the Lodges, in their wagon pulled by the third Ryan draft horse. Zeb came next, riding Kapucha. He led the fourth of the draft horses, which served as a packhorse. Behind Zeb rode the three dragoons of the rear guard.

The convoy snaked out of Washington onto the Natchez Road. Two hours later they stopped at Mount Locust Inn to water the horses. The light rain had stopped and the sky was clearing. Everyone seemed to be in good spirits.

A courier galloped in and handed Captain Morrison an envelope. Zeb watched as the captain read the message, then wrote a note and handed it back to the courier. The captain surveyed the group standing around and stretching and ordered the sergeant to reassemble the convoy. As they re-formed, Captain Morrison checked the members once again. He stopped to talk with Mr. Ebersole and Mr. Swanson. "I don't like the look of your horses. Have you been exercising them as I asked?"

"We rode them every day since the day you mentioned it," Mr. Ebersole said. "These are good horses. We brought them with us all the way from Pittsburgh."

"*What?* You mean those horses have been idle on a flatboat for two months or more?" Captain Morrison demanded.

"Yes, but—"

"Enough! If you are smart, you will go back now, while you have the chance. Those horses will never make it. If you decide to continue and if you cannot keep up, we will have to leave you wherever we are."

When the captain reached the missionary family, he was still angry with Ebersole and Swanson. Mrs. Lodge was in the back of the wagon sorting through their supplies. The two girls sat on the bench with their father. They looked up, their eyes wide with fright as Captain Morrison pulled the horse to a stop next to the wagon.

"This is your last chance," he said impatiently. "You've got a much better horse now, and the wagon has been repaired, but I'm still afraid the wagon won't make it. You can easily go back to Washington from here without an escort. Surely you have more sense than those two fools up in front." He waited a moment. When they did not respond, he said, "If, however, you decide to continue with us and you break down anywhere between here and Yowani, I will have to leave you and continue with the rest of the convoy, just as I told them. I cannot be responsible for you."

The captain nodded to the sergeant, who waved his arm and shouted, "Move out!" The convoy moved forward once again.

When they reached their campsite the first night, the dragoons immediately put up their tents in a neat row. The civilians formed a loose circle around the campsite. Zeb helped the Lodge family put up the new tent and then loaned them the Spanish army shovel to dig a trench around it. They rolled out the ground cloth and put their meager possessions inside.

The dragoons were busy digging the army latrine and making the communal cook fire. Everyone pitched in except Ebersole and Swanson.

Hannah and Zeb collected kindling for the fire, while two of the dragoons cut wood.

They had all carried some food with them: salted meat to be cooked over the fire, white potatoes and yams, and winter vegetables such as cabbage and collards. Everyone had brought bread, since they would see no more until they reached Nashville. Once they ran out of food, they would have to stop at the stands, the little makeshift inns located about twenty-five miles apart on the road. If they were going to keep the schedule Captain Morrison had set, they would seldom have time or opportunity to hunt.

Hannah and Zeb searched for mud to pat around the potatoes they were planning to bake in the cook fire. But the soil was still too sandy. They wet the potatoes, and Hannah rolled them into the fire with a piece of kindling. She looked at Zeb and grinned. "Remember those wonderful baked potatoes the night we crossed the Duck River?" she asked.

"Course," he replied. "I thought they were the best potatoes I'd ever eaten!"

After they ate, each person went to the stream and washed his or her own tin dish, pots, and utensils with sand and water. But Swanson and Ebersole didn't bother. *Are they gonna eat off dirty plates tomorrow morning?* Zeb wondered. *Maybe they think someone'll wash the gear for them.*

The McAllisters had set up their tent next to Zeb and his grampa. They watched as Ebersole and Swanson stacked their dirty plates and pots and put them back inside their tent.

"They may give out before the horses do," Cracker Ryan observed. "They're bound to get sick if they don't clean their cooking gear. They may need your services before morning, Dr. McAllister."

Captain Morrison walked around the campsite and talked with each group. When he got to the McAllisters and Zeb and his grampa, the old man asked him, "What do you think will happen to Dancey Moore?"

"I have news for you. I received a message at Mount Locust Inn. I have mixed feelings about the news, so I wanted to wait until we set up for the night to tell you."

"Oh, no!" Hannah cried. "Don't tell us that Moore escaped!"

"No, Hannah. The territorial judge felt that there was not enough evidence to convict him for Lonnie Champ's death. His lawyer convinced the judge that no one could prove that it was murder, so Moore was convicted on lesser charges. He was sentenced to ten years in prison doing hard labor. Those men he had with him were sentenced to five years."

"That should take care of him for a while, Hannah," Zeb said.

"But Captain Morrison, you don't seem particularly happy," Cracker Ryan said.

"I'm not. The judge wrote that he thought it was a nice irony, having Moore and his men work out their hard labor sentence mucking out the stables at Fort Dearborn."

Cracker Ryan sagged. "Oh, no!" he said.

"What's the matter with that?" Zeb asked. "I think it's funny. Serves him right."

Cracker Ryan said, "Dancey Moore is a scoundrel, a thief, and probably anything else we might name, but he does know horses, and he knows how to dicker as few people do."

Hannah interrupted. "But I don't see—"

"He and his men will do that job better than it has ever been done. They'll bathe and brush and currycomb the horses. They'll have them oiled and shined and ready for parade, particularly the officers' horses, the sergeants' horses, and the horses of the men in charge of keepin' watch on them."

Captain Morrison nodded. "You're right. It won't be long before they'll be breaking horses for the dragoons and maybe helping in the training some of the new recruits. We have a lot of new recruits now and too few experienced men to train them."

Zeb shrugged. "So he'll be doin' something he knows about, something he likes. He'll still be in prison."

"But not for long, unless I miss my guess," Captain Morrison said. "He has contact with a lawyer, which means he has access to his bank account. Can you imagine what a temptation a bribe of five hundred or maybe a thousand dollars would be to some of those new recruits? I sent a letter back to the commanding officer, asking him to talk with the judge. I hope I'm not too late."

"Too late?" Hannah asked.

"If they do escape, they can't go back to Natchez. They'll either go to New Orleans or they'll come north…up the Nashville Road!"

Zeb looked down the dark road.

"Unfortunately," Captain Morrison said, "if this happens, they will be mounted on excellent horses, in good condition. They will surely be armed. And Dancey Moore wants revenge. He's furious with you, Hannah, for fooling him."

Hannah's mother pulled her close. "What will we do?"

"I doubt he'll attack the convoy, but we'll double the watch at night. Once you're at Yowani, he can't hurt you."

Dr. McAllister put his arms around Hannah's shoulders. "He's right. We'll talk with the Miko. He'll never let Moore within a mile of Yowani."

Dr. and Mrs. McAllister walked away with Hannah between them, the three of them talking quietly.

"We'll look after Hannah," Zeb said.

"And what about the sergeant?" Cracker Ryan asked Captain Morrison.

"Of course, I regret now that I let him go. That combination of Moore and Scruggs is a very dangerous one. If Moore does escape and the sergeant joins him, they'll be hard to stop. The army has a number of people in Natchez Under-The-Hill looking for the sergeant."

The captain looked down at the old Ryan camping tent. "I'm glad you loaned your new tent to the missionary family. I know it must sound to you that I'm too rough on them, but I had been hoping that they would decide not go. Mark my words. That wagon will break down, and there is nothing that anyone will be able to do for them."

The captain touched his hat. "Good night."

The next day, the horses ridden by Ebersole and Swanson were obviously tired. The convoy had slowed and stopped more frequently to rest, but it was clear on the fourth night that the merchant's horses couldn't make it. "We will reach Brashear's Stand by noon tomorrow," Captain Morrison told them. "If you can't keep up tomorrow, try to make it to the stand. At least you'll have a place to stay until you can make other arrangements."

"Other arrangements?" Ebersole asked.

"You may find someone willing to sell you a horse," Captain Morrison said. "A horse in good condition. Or maybe with a month of daily conditioning, you might be able to get those four horses into good shape."

"But how will we catch up with the convoy?"

"You won't. You will have to go alone, like most of the others on the Nashville Road. I wish you had turned back at Mount Locust."

"You can't do this to us! I'll write to your commanding officer."

"Good. He'll be pleased to know that I am carrying out his orders."

The convoy left the next morning, with Ebersole and Swanson far behind, and arrived at Brashear's Stand about noon, where they stopped and had their noon meal. They had just finished eating when Ebersole and Swanson arrived. Their horses were walking slowly with their heads down, their necks and flanks lathered.

The two men immediately began to negotiate for horses. Ebersole approached Cracker Ryan. "I understand you are a horse trader and that the four draft horses are yours," he said.

When the old man nodded, Ebersole continued. "I'd like to buy 'em from you."

"They're being used. How can I possibly sell them?"

"You can leave the squaw, her kid, and that white man who's with 'em here at the stand. They're probably used to a lot worse than this. We'll give the kid some money for that big horse she's riding. That horse could pull the wagon and we'll give you such a good price, you won't mind givin' up whatever you're carryin' on the packhorses. Whaddya say?"

"Mr. Ebersole," Cracker Ryan growled, "up to a minute ago I was feelin' a little sorry for you two. Now I wouldn't sell you *one* of those horses, much less four. No matter what the price!"

"I know you're a horse trader, Ryan. That's just a good dickering line you're usin'. But money talks. I'll offer you five hundred dollars a horse!"

Cracker Ryan began to uncoil his whip. "Do you know why I'm called Cracker Ryan?"

Ebersole shouted, "All right! Five hundred was low. Seven fifty?... A thousand?"

The old man stepped back and gave the whip a little flip with his wrist. The end snaked out and took a leaf off a nearby tree.

Cracker Ryan held up his other hand. "Please, Mr. Ebersole. Don't say another word."

Ebersole raised his fist and shook it at Cracker Ryan. "You're crazy, you old fool...."

The whip arm came back and the tip end picked off another leaf. "Don't say another word."

Ebersole slunk away, muttering under his breath.

Dr. McAllister appeared at Cracker Ryan's side. "We heard all that. Thank you. Some of the soldiers told us that those two were boasting how they sold Monongahela whiskey to the Indians all the way down from Pittsburgh in trade for pelts and skins. They boasted how easy it was to fool the Indians once they had a little whiskey in them."

Cracker Ryan coiled up the whip. "They'll probably lose all that money before they leave Brashear's Stand. It'll serve 'em right."

The convoy packed up and started up the highway. They stopped in the early evening and camped at the edge of a meadow near the Pearl River.

CHAPTER EIGHTEEN

Earthquake

December 16, 1811

Zeb was shaken out of a deep sleep. He started to reach for his boots when his bedroll shook again. "All right! All right!" he whispered. "I'm up."

His grampa sat up. "What's goin' on?"

The ground below them trembled violently. "What was that? Grampa, did you feel that?"

He tied his boot laces together and threw them around his neck, the boots dangling on his chest. He crawled out of the tent and stood barefoot to stare at the field of grass. A quarter moon was up, right over his head. *Must be just a little after midnight,* he noted. The ground below the grass was rippling like the surface of a big lake in a rainstorm, but he felt no wind. The ground trembled again and he heard branches snap and crash to the ground behind him.

His grampa crawled out next to him. "Earthquake!" he shouted. "C'mon! We've got to get away from these trees...."

They ran barefoot toward the meadow.

"Let's go get the horses!" his grampa shouted. "We'll take 'em to the center of the field."

Now Zeb could hear great explosive snaps from the forest behind them, followed by a long *whoosh* as the giant trees crashed in the forest. The horses were neighing and someone was screaming in fear or in pain.

A strange odor wafted around the woods and the field. Zeb wrinkled his nose. *Almost like rotten eggs,* he thought, *or like the smell when you strike flint with steel.*

The dragoons had already begun moving the frightened horses to the center of the meadow. Zeb ran to help. He untied the reins from the tree limbs where the horses were tethered and soon had Kapucha's and Christmas's leads in his hands. His grampa was leading Andy and one of the draft horses to the center of the meadow. The shaking seemed to have stopped and the horses were beginning to calm down a bit.

The dragoons immediately cut pieces of wood to stake out their horses. Zeb was impressed with how calmly and quickly they handled emergencies, as if they had practiced what to do in case of an earthquake. But he knew that there hadn't been an earthquake in this whole area in his lifetime, and no one had ever told him of one happening near here in the past.

Zeb's grampa took the lead lines from him, and Zeb ran to where the Lodges were camping. The little girls sat in the bed of the wagon, peering wide-eyed over the edge. The younger one screamed, "Mama! Mama! Mama!" Zeb stepped between the traces and pulled the wagon out to the field.

Reverend Lodge and his wife pulled up the stakes of the tent, dragging it as they hurried behind the wagon into the meadow.

Zeb's grampa ran up, grabbed one of the traces, and helped pull it to the center of the meadow. Then he pointed to their gear. "Quick, load our pack baskets onto the horses. Then get the small ax out and make some stakes. Be careful. Stay only at the edge of the woods. I think the earthquake is over, but some trees could still fall."

Zeb ran to help move the frightened horses.

Just as Zeb turned to get the ax, the earth began to shake again. Zeb was thrown to the ground. He was surprised to feel the vibrations through his hands. He looked up as the huge trees lashed back and forth.

Someone shouted, "River's risin'!"

They all stared in horror at the other end of the meadow as the Pearl River began to overflow its banks. Zeb struggled back to his feet as the water rushed across the field. With a sudden hiss and a cloud of steam, the water extinguished the hot coals from the smoldering campfire.

When everyone looked for a place to run, Captain Morrison shouted, "Hold your positions! There is no higher ground!" He looked down at the water, now ankle deep. "I don't think this will get much deeper." He looked toward the river. "The earthquake must have blocked up the river downstream, but the water pressure will soon break the logjam."

Hannah and her parents splashed through the water toward Zeb. Their shoes tied around their necks, they carried their bedrolls and other belongings over their heads.

When the shaking stopped, Captain Morrison sloshed through the water to the group gathered in the center of the field. "We learned about earthquakes at West Point Military Academy," he told them. "These are probably aftershocks. We will have a number of them. I believe that each one will be a little less strong than the previous one, but could still be very dangerous." He paused for a moment, then said, "We'll wait until morning and if the river doesn't rise any higher, we'll continue our journey north."

"But that's impossible!" Dr. McAllister said. "How can we travel under these conditions?"

Captain Morrison replied, "We will move north at daylight. There is nothing to be gained by staying here." He gestured around him. "The campsite is covered with water. There is no room for discussion."

Zeb began to feel the water moving in the other direction across his bare feet. Slowly, the water drained back into the riverbed.

Mrs. Lodge climbed up into the wagon with the girls and held the little one in her arms, rocking her and talking to her quietly.

The missionary tried to fold the wet tent. Zeb took the other end, and together they draped it over a tree limb to dry.

It was barely light when the captain informed them that they would be moving out within the hour. "There is still some venison from last night," he said. "Eat what you want. We'll leave the rest for other travelers."

Zeb folded the still-damp tent and tied it to the other bundles on the packhorse. He tacked up Kapucha for the trip north. Hannah and her parents were saddling their horses. The dragoons had their horses ready to go.

In the dark forest, it was impossible to see the sun rise, but they could sense the new dawn as they prepared to move out.

They lined up and moved onto the Nashville Road once again.

CHAPTER NINETEEN

The Cypress Swamp

December 16, 1811

L ess than an hour later, after winding around tree limbs now strewn across the trail, they reached a sharp curve in the road. The dragoon sergeant suddenly raised his hand and the convoy came to an uneasy stop. The sergeant dismounted, looping the reins over the saddle. He walked slowly forward and then stopped and stood with his hands on his hips, looking around the turn in the road. The captain, who had been at the rear of the convoy, cantered up to the sergeant.

"What is going on, sergeant?" he demanded.

The sergeant pointed to a place out of sight of the rest of the convoy, where the road curved sharply to the left.

The captain dismounted.

Zeb vaulted off Kapucha and ran up to where the sergeant and the captain were standing. He couldn't believe what he was seeing. The cypress swamp that had been on both sides of the road when they had traveled down the trail just a few months ago now seemed to have swallowed up the road itself. The road disappeared into the swamp and came out the other side. For a distance of about ten wagon lengths, there was no road at all!

"Earthquake must have done this," Captain Morrison muttered. He looked around. "Perfect place for an ambush."

The sergeant signaled the men, who dismounted and took positions on either side of the road. The sergeant and the Captain remounted, moving quickly up and down the line. Zeb and his grampa pulled their rifles from the saddle holsters.

The captain told the Lodges to lie down in the bed of the wagon.

Zeb looked around the forest. Trees were down everywhere. Many just leaned on upright trees. But the big cypress trees in the swamp—with their wide lower trunks and their strange roots half out of the water—were all upright.

One of the dragoons changed into a green stable jacket and gray hat so he would be harder to spot in the woods and slipped into the forest. After twenty minutes, he crossed the highway behind them and went into the forest on the other side. The captain's horse skittered when he suddenly appeared a half hour later at Captain Morrison's side. "There is no evidence of horses or men on this side of the swamp, sir," he said.

Zeb heard a click as Cracker Ryan uncocked his rifle. Zeb took a deep breath and did the same. The Lodges sat up in their rickety wagon.

"Sergeant," the captain ordered, "have two of the men ride through that swamp to the other side. We need to know how deep it is and what the bottom is like. I want them to cut long poles and test the bottom in front of them and to each side as they move forward. There could be a ditch or a new channel underneath that water. If they find deep water, they are to turn around and come back."

As a pair of soldiers urged their horses into the water, the horses sidled along the edge of the swamp, refusing at first to go in. The green slime on top of the water made it impossible to see what was underneath. The soldiers urged them forward again, and finally the horses placed one careful foot in front of the other into the thick muddy water, one horse slightly ahead of the other.

The men moved the horses forward a few steps, stopped them, prodded with the poles, and then moved forward again. When they had gone no more than the length of a wagon, the man in front pushed the pole into deeper water, but he was able to touch the bottom. He moved the pole to the right and then to the left, checking an area about three feet wide. His horse stepped into the deeper water, the green slime reaching the dragoon's knees. When the horse struggled to move ahead, the dragoon stopped him, checked once again with the pole, and then moved forward. The soldiers urged the horses on, stopping to prod and check until they finally emerged on the other side.

They turned the horses around and carefully crossed the swamp again. One of them reported to the sergeant. "Bottom seems difficult for the horse, Sergeant," he said. "Thick mud, I would guess. But underneath the mud, the bottom is solid. The water is not too deep for a big horse, but it might cause problems for the wagon."

The captain told the sergeant to send three of the men to the other side. He ordered the scout to go with them and check the forest. Everyone stared at the green water, watching to see if anything broke through the surface.

The scout came back in about an hour with the news that there was no sign of outlaws or anyone else in the forest.

The sergeant ordered the men to lead the civilians on horseback across the swamp. One by one they struggled with the deep water and the muddy bottom. The minister and his family waited behind. When the captain sent three of the soldiers back, two of them put the little girls in front of them on their saddles and rode them across the swamp.

Mary, the seven year old, seemed very confident on the horse. She held on to the mane and smiled up at the soldier. Beth, the five year old, had both hands on the pommel and kept twisting to look back at her mother. The missionary's wife rode behind one of the soldiers. She waved at Mary reassuringly.

After crossing the swamp, some of the soldiers stood guard while the others scraped the slime off the horses' legs and bellies and checked them for leeches. They lifted the horse's feet and pried the packed mud and stones out of the hooves. Zeb and Hannah followed their example and took care of the rest of the horses.

Now all that remained was the missionary wagon. Reverend Lodge clucked the big draft horse forward and into the green slime. When the horse stepped into the deep water, the farm wagon floated behind him. One of the back wheels was at an angle and scraped against the wagon bed. It looked like the wheel was coming off. The horse could not move forward.

Without saying anything, Zeb mounted Christmas and Cracker Ryan mounted Andy. Zeb walked his horse into the green slime and the missionary climbed on Christmas behind him. Zeb then moved Christmas over next to the wagon. "Grab that saddle," he told the missionary. "If we can't move it, we'll have to cut the wagon loose and you'll want that to ride the horse."

"If you have to cut the wagon loose," the missionary said, holding the saddle under one arm, "I'll have to come back and get the rest of the things. They're all we have."

"That's what we'll do," Zeb said. He left the missionary with his family. Then he and his grampa maneuvered their horses to either side of the draft horse. With his boots hanging around his neck and his socks in the boots, Zeb slipped off Christmas and squished through the mud to hitch Andy and Christmas to the wagon on either side of the draft horse.

Zeb and his grampa nodded to each other and slowly began to move forward. The two rear wheels of the wagon, now completely stuck in the mud, came off, and the wagon box tore away from the chassis. The box broke into pieces. The Lodges' belongings disappeared under the green slime. The three horses pulled the broken chassis and the two front wheels out onto the north side of the swamp.

"Oh, no!" the missionary cried, leaping into the swamp. He struggled through the muck toward the place where the wagon box was last seen. He thrust one arm into the water, his head turned to the side, his face green with slime.

Zeb waded out and stood next to him. "We must go back, Mr. Lodge. It's too dangerous out here. If your feet get stuck in this thick mud, we may not be able to help you."

"But I must find them," the minister gasped.

Zeb put his arm around the Reverend Lodge and turned him toward the shore. The minister kept looking over his shoulder, "All will be lost. I must find them...."

"Whatever you have lost can probably be replaced at Yowani."

When they got back on the dry road, the minister stood before his family. His clothes, his hands, and the side of his face were covered with green slime. "I'm sorry," he said, still gasping for breath. "We won't be able to start the way I had hoped. I'll have to contact the Foreign Board of Missions after all."

He looked up at the sky, visible now through the winter lacework of bare tree limbs. "Maybe it was wrong to believe that this was to be my mission," he said in a low voice. "Losing that box was a sign."

Dr. McAllister put his hand on the missionary's shoulder. "Don't worry, we can help you with whatever you need."

The missionary sagged. "You don't understand. There was a box with ten Bibles in that wagon."

*The two rear wheels of the wagon came off and
the wagon box broke into pieces.*

Hannah looked up at him. "We have lots of Bibles at Yowani," she said. "The traveling preachers leave them with us."

"You have Bibles at Yowani?"

Hannah nodded. "My friend Nashoba and some of the others are trying to translate them. They don't agree on the best way to write the translation yet."

"Translate the Bible! Into Choctaw?"

"Nashoba taught me one verse in Choctaw." She looked off into the forest as if she were trying to remember. She quoted,

chim okla hak osh
um okla cha,
chin Chitokaka ak osh
an Chitokaka ha chi hoke.

"And that means?"

And thy people
shall be my people
and thy God
my God.

The Reverend Lodge looked toward the sky once again and said, "Thank you."

Little Beth looked up at her father, tugging on his pant leg. "Will you be able to find my doll?" she asked.

Hannah squatted down next to Beth. "We have lots of dolls at Yowani, too. You will have a new one when you get to your new home."

The captain walked over to the missionary family. "Now what?" he said. "I told you, I can't wait for you. I'm sorry, but I simply cannot wait."

153

Without saying a word, Zeb picked up Beth, put her on Kapucha at the front of the saddle, and then mounted the horse, wrapping his arms around her. Mary moved over to Christmas. Dr. McAllister helped Hannah mount and then helped Mary get up on the horse behind Hannah. Reverend Lodge saddled the draft horse, and he and his wife mounted. She sat behind him.

The captain stared at them, then nodded.

Hannah and Mary rode toward the convoy. Zeb and Beth followed until they were riding alongside Hannah, with Zeb still leading the packhorse. The Reverend and Mrs. Lodge urged the draft horse forward until they were behind the convoy.

Captain Morrison trotted his horse back and forth behind the group, then rode up next to Zeb. "That maneuver took some planning," he said gruffly. "Whoever anticipated the situation and carried out the plan ought to be in the army."

Hannah turned and saluted Zeb. "Nice going, Sergeant D'Evereux." She grinned.

The captain announced to the convoy, "We will proceed on until we find a dry area, where we will camp for the night."

"Yes," Dr. McAllister agreed. "We must leave this place as soon as possible. People who stay around the swamps often come down with the fever."

They had traveled north for about an hour when they came to a place where the road was blocked by a number of large fallen trees. The sergeant led the way into the woods, expecting to find an easy way around. But it was not to be. The group had only proceeded a few hundred yards into the woods when another series of aftershocks slammed more trees to the ground around them.

Hearing a strange creaking noise, Zeb looked up. The tops of the trees were whipping back and forth like deep grass in a windy meadow. *Some of these aftershocks seem as strong as the earthquake,* Zeb thought.

The sergeant called two men to him. When they dismounted and started to walk through the forest looking for a way out, they startled a doe, which turned and fled. The two men followed her.

When they returned, the sergeant informed the captain that they had found a route back to the trail, but they would need to cut some tree limbs so the horses could get through.

The group waited in nervous silence as the dragoons chopped away at the limbs. Finally the sergeant and the captain walked their horses through the opening and beckoned to the group to follow quickly, before another aftershock. They passed single file through the forest and then finally back onto the Nashville Road.

Wherever the road was wide enough, Hannah and Zeb rode side by side. It seemed to reassure Beth, who often looked around Zeb to see if her mother and father were still behind her. Sometimes Zeb or Hannah told the girls stories of their exciting adventures together, and other times they traveled in comfortable silence or made faces at each other to liven up the long journey.

When they reached an open area next to a wide creek, Captain Morrison raised his hand and the convoy pulled in. The group could see smooth, flat pebbles at the bottom of the shallow river, but the water was a little cloudy in places from the periodic tremors. They set up camp.

Captain Morrison informed them that this was a small tributary to the Big Black River. They were near the Choctaw village of Yockanookany.

Zeb smiled, remembering that first day at Yockanookany Village. He met Hannah's eyes, his smile a little sad. *It'll be hard to leave her at Yowani,* he realized, *as much as I want to get home. I'm gonna miss her.*

The soldiers waded the army horses into the river to wash off the dried green slime and, once again, to check for leeches. Zeb and Hannah joined the soldiers and washed the other horses in the cold river water.

As soon as the horses were taken care of, Zeb returned to the river to bathe. He found the minister there, stripped to his underwear. The two of them sat in the cold water, scrubbing their clothes with lye soap and then trying to get the slime off their legs with sand.

They didn't talk. The Reverend Lodge hummed to himself and Zeb thought of home. *What will it be like,* he wondered, *to ride down that steep meadow into the farmyard, bringing Grampa home? What will it be like to see Mama again?*

CHAPTER TWENTY

Yowani

December 18, 1811

By the late afternoon of the second day after they left the little river near Yockanookany Village, Zeb knew they were near Yowani. The Natchez Road was wider here. A short way down the road he began to see the simple fences built to keep Dr. McAllister's special cattle with cowpox from wandering away or being poached by outlaws or boaters. They passed the Choctaw Council House where he had met Nashoba for the first time.

Many trees had fallen here, too, but he could see that the Choctaw had been busy cutting and moving those that were in the road. Around the outside of the village, Zeb could see several trees whose main roots had snapped. Some of them had not yet fallen, their upper branches caught in the branches of other trees.

Hannah, with Mary riding behind her, moved up to the head of the convoy. Christmas acted as if he wanted to run. But Zeb knew that it was Hannah who wanted to run. *This is the place she thinks of as home. Except for Katie Culpepper, this is where all of her friends are.* Captain Morrison smiled and motioned her on.

When she reached the entrance to Yowani Village and the Medical Research Station, the gate was open. Isushi, the old

Choctaw who had been Hannah's guide and mentor, was at the gate. "*Aiok panchi!*" he called. "Welcome!"

"Isushi!" Hannah shouted, trying to control Christmas. "You were waiting for us! You knew we were coming!"

"We have had braves watching you for the last two days, so you would be safe. The village is happy to see you and your family back among us."

He pointed through the open gate. "Go now. The *Miko* and the *Alikchi* are waiting to greet you."

Hannah and Mary trotted through the gate with the convoy trailing far behind. It was almost dark. As Zeb moved into the village, he could see the cook fires glowing, and he smelled roasting game and baked yams. He was starved.

The convoy dismounted and stood in front of the Miko and the Alikchi.

"The Miko is the village chief," Dr. McAllister told the captain, "and the Alikchi is the medicine man and spiritual leader."

"Aiok Panchi!" the Miko said. "We welcome you all to Yowani. We welcome back our friend, Doctor McAllister, and his family. We have good news for you, Doctor. We still have six cows of the original herd. Our Alikchi tells me that some have cowpox."

Dr. McAllister took the Miko's hand in his and thanked him. "I want you to meet Mr. David Lodge, his wife Mary, and their two children. Mr. Lodge is a missionary. He hopes that he and his family may stay here in Yowani."

The Miko nodded. "Welcome to Yowani," he said. "For tonight, at least, why don't you and your family stay in the cabin next to Doctor McAllister? It was built for medical research staff, but there is no one else here now."

"Thank you, sir," David Lodge said. "We have a lot to be thankful for."

"That is true for all of us," the Miko said.

Dr. McAllister put his hand on Zeb's shoulder. "I know that it is not necessary to introduce this man whom you call Brave Horse, *Isuba Nakni.* Just as he is a brother to you, he is now like a son to us."

"Welcome home, Isuba Nakni."

Dr. McAllister continued, "I want you to meet his grandfather, Daniel Ryan."

Zeb's grampa moved forward. "You have greatly honored me and my family by making my grandson one of yours."

The Miko said, "We know of you, Mr. Ryan. We witnessed your grandson gentling a horse, Kapucha, and he told us where he had learned to do that. We are happy he was able to find you in Natchez. You are welcome in our village, now and whenever you travel on this trail."

As the old man stepped back, Dr. McAllister continued, "I would like to present to you Captain Morrison of the Fort Dearborn Dragoons."

The Miko turned to Captain Morrison. "We have watched you for several days and know that you and your soldiers were guarding our friends. We invite you to stay here with us and participate tomorrow in the Aiok Panchi festivities."

Captain Morrison saluted the Miko. "It is an honor for me and for my men to meet you, sir. Hannah suspected that your braves were there in the forest," he said, "but we never saw them." Then he continued, "I wish we could accept your invitation, sir, but we must be in Nashville before the new year. That is a long trip."

The Miko nodded. "Whatever you wish, of course. I am sure, however, if you decide to stay, that you will be able to travel that distance easily. We are told that the army is already clearing the road through Chickasaw country. We expect them to get to Choctaw country by the new moon. A festival will give us an opportunity to know each other."

The captain turned to his sergeant. They conferred quietly for a moment. He then addressed the Miko. "Your information about the road clearing is very welcome indeed. We will stay for the festivities, then. We, too, would like to get to know you better. I will give my men leave tomorrow so they may relax and enjoy their time with your people."

He looked around the village. "If you will show us where we may put up our tents and graze the horses...."

The Miko motioned with his hand and two mounted nakni appeared. One of the braves was Running Bear. Zeb grinned up at him, remembering the strange horse race that happened that last time he was in Yowani. Running Bear grinned back.

It was like no horse race I had ever seen, Zeb recalled. *The horses that the Choctaw nakni and I rode that day had never been ridden before.*

The two nakni led the soldiers and Zeb to the edge of a large meadow. Zeb could see goalposts at each end of the field. *What will the dragoons think of ishtaboli?* This field was not as large as the one at Yockanookany Village, but Zeb was sure there would be plenty of room for the games and the horse racing. He wondered if he would have a chance to race against Running Bear again.

Zeb went back to where the horses were tethered and led the packhorse to the campsite. Because the Lodges were to sleep in a cabin, Zeb and his grampa would use the tent tonight for the first time. He dismounted, pulled the tent off the horse, and stretched it out on the ground. He cut two saplings for tent posts. Once he had the tent up, he crawled inside, unrolled the ground cloth on the dirt floor of the tent, and then backed out.

He saw his grampa and the Alikchi walking and talking as if they had known each other a long time. The Miko was moving from group to group. When he got to Zeb, he said, "Isuba Nakni, do you have everything you need?"

"Yes, sir, thank you, I do. But I wonder, is Nashoba here?"

"No. He and his father are at Yockanookany Village, visiting with the Alikchi there. They should be back early in the morning. His father has not yet recovered from his wounds. They will tell you about it tomorrow."

He pointed back to the smoke coming from the village cook fires. "The food is there for each of you to take as you wish. It is not much. Save your appetite for tomorrow when we shall have a celebration. Isuba Nakni, you and the others may leave your large horses in this fenced field." The Miko left Zeb to go and talk with the soldiers.

Zeb was suddenly very hungry and tired. The venison was suspended over the glowing coals, still cooking slowly. Zeb held the meat with a sharp stick and cut off a strip with his knife. He walked back and forth, too impatient to let it cool, eating little pieces and burning his mouth.

He was glad to finally spend a night in the large new tent that Mr. Yadkin had made for him so long ago. He and the others had brought Hannah and her family to Yowani, and now Zeb was starting to feel like he was really going home.

Zeb awoke early the next morning. His grampa was still asleep next to him. *This is the coldest morning yet,* Zeb thought. He sighed, then dressed and grabbed his coat.

Outside, he looked up at the bleak, bare limbs of the trees against the early morning sky. *Winter is coming and we're goin' home!*

After breakfast at the cook fires, he walked past the Ishtaboli field. Someone had decorated the goalposts with garlands of evergreen.

By late morning, venison and wild pig hung over the cook fires. Zeb's stomach growled at the wonderful aroma of roasting meat wafting through the village.

The little children, Mary and Beth Lodge among them, played on the ponies at one end of the field. Their screams and laughter reminded Zeb of church picnics back in Franklin.

He watched footraces and wrestling matches and wondered what Lonnie would have thought of them. Zeb sat on the top rail of the fence to watch the games. He kept looking back at the village, hoping to see some sign of Nashoba and his father.

One of the young dragoons, whom Zeb had met the night before, climbed up and sat on the rail next to him. He watched the games with Zeb in silence for a while. Then he said, "Hear they gonna have a horse race."

Zeb nodded. "They'll have a horse race," he said, "like nothin' you have ever seen. Best to stay out of it."

"Doubt they's a race I hain't seen," the soldier said. "I wouldn't mind a-racin' some. Course, army horses ain't built fer speed, and mine's a bit peaked, but I'd race my horse anyway, if'n I could find some feller wanted to race."

"Maybe some of the other dragoons—"

"Naw, they don't wanna race. And besides, they don't got no money to bet. I noticed you always have a little money when we get to the stands."

Zeb tried to keep from smiling. *This soldier is trying to fool me with his Kaintuck accent, and his claim that army horses can't run fast. Just a short time ago,* Zeb thought, *I would have been doing the same thing.*

The soldier gestured at Christmas tethered to the fence rail. "How come you got that big horse tethered? He got any speed? Somebody said you think he pretty fast. I ain't seen airy one like that'n afore."

Zeb shook his head and, playing the same game, said, "Christmas is here for Hannah, if'n she wants him. She's off someplace with her parents right now. Speed? She's no faster than you'd expect."

"What about it? You wanna race?"

Zeb shook his head. "Sorry," he said. "I've got responsibilities. Can't do it."

"Yer not afeered a' racin' are you?

"Maybe, in a way, I am. Can't take a chance."

Zeb looked up at the big horse. *Christmas, I hope you didn't hear that.*

If my horse fell, he continued to himself, *the way he did last time, I could be badly hurt. Then how would Grampa get all these horses home by himself? What would happen to the farm?*

The young soldier shook his head. *Probably shocked,* Zeb thought, *that anyone would admit they're afraid to race.*

Then Zeb heard a shriek. The children at the far end of the field were trying to catch a runaway pony. Clinging to the pony's back was Mary, her legs stiff, her body flung back, and her fists full of the pony's mane. As the pony galloped past Zeb and the dragoon, Mary looked at Zeb in terror. Zeb waved to her to bend over and get closer to the horse.

Zeb leaped off the rail, flung the reins over Christmas' head, and vaulted up on him. Christmas thundered after the runaway Choctaw pony.

The pony slipped and, for a moment, Zeb thought it might fall. *If she doesn't know to jump, Mary could be crushed.* The surefooted little animal recovered quickly though, and it started down the other side of the field, gradually slowing from a dead run to an easy canter. Mary threw her body forward. She bent her legs and tightened them around the pony's flanks, her head close to the horse's neck.

Zeb cut in front of the goalposts and raced alongside the pony. He reached out and grabbed Mary around the waist, yanked her off the pony, and swung her astride Christmas.

He slowed Christmas and caught his breath. When the big horse finally slowed to a walk, Mary turned and looked up at him. "I wasn't scared!" she said, still gasping for air.

Zeb smiled. "You like ridin' fast, do you?"

She nodded. She put her hands out to hold onto the reins. "Can I ride Christmas sometime?"

Zeb shook his head. "We won't be here after tomorrow. But I hope to come back someday. By then you'll be ready to ride anything. You just listen to Hannah and do whatever she tells you. She rides better than just about anybody I know."

When they got back to the other side of the field, Zeb handed Mary down to her mother. Zeb's grampa was reassuring and calming the missionary. "She's goin' to be an excellent rider, Mr. Lodge. She has a natural gift for ridin', the way Hannah does."

Zeb untacked Christmas and let the big horse loose in the pasture with the other horses. He walked back to the rail where the young dragoon was still sitting. Zeb climbed up and sat on the top rail next to him.

The young man looked at him a long while, then said, "Thanks a lot."

Zeb turned to him. "For what?"

"For not makin' a fool of me when I wanted to race you."

Zeb chuckled. "Funny, you seem to have lost your Kaintuck accent."

"I talk like that so folks I race against think they're takin' advantage of me. They think I don't know nothin'."

And if you ever try to sell them a horse, Zeb thought, *they'll check his mouth again and again. They won't trust you.*

He reached out and yanked Mary off the pony.

Zeb jumped off the fence. "I'm going over to the McAllister cabin," he said, "to see if they have news of Nashoba and his father."

"You ain't gonna stay for the horse race?"

"Naw." Zeb smiled. "I a'ready done that oncet."

He stopped at his tent and picked up his small saddlebag. After unwrapping several layers of oilskin, he pulled out his leather-bound notebook.

He was about to climb the stairs to knock on the door when he saw Nashoba striding toward him from the Choctaw Council House. He, too, was carrying a book.

Nashoba and Zeb hugged and pounded each other on the back, then stood back and grinned. "I'll bet you're anxious to see Hannah and her family," Zeb said.

"I have already seen them. I asked Dr. McAllister to come to see my father."

"Will he be able to help?"

"He isn't sure. My father was wounded with a Muskogee spear. The wound was not deep, but it is now swollen and red. His body is hot. The Alikchi is trying to help. I am hoping that Dr. McAllister might help, too."

Hannah opened the door. She motioned them in and turned back to walk in ahead of them. She had tears in her eyes.

"Is everything all right?" Zeb asked.

Hannah's mother pointed to a place on the floor, near the fireplace. "Sit down, Zeb, Nashoba. We're just talking about how much we will all miss you when you leave tomorrow, Zeb. I can never thank you enough...."

Zeb shook his head. "Please. You don't need to. I'm not sure I would have made it without Hannah—"

Hannah interrupted. "Please promise to come back, Zeb."

Nashoba, seated on the floor, leaned back against the log

wall. "I, too, hope you will return. I will be attending the Jefferson School next year. I wish you would consider it as well."

He handed Zeb a sheet of paper. "Jefferson School gave me a list of books to read. I've read many of them already. I copied it for you."

Zeb looked at the list, then shrugged. "I've thought a lot about it. I really wish I could get more schooling, but now with the problems at the farm, I doubt I'll get away for a couple of years."

Nashoba reached his hand out and offered Zeb the book he was carrying. "These are the writings of John Locke and Jean Jacques Rousseau on the natural rights of man. It's the book I was reading when you arrived at Yowani Council House. I've finished it and want you to have it. It's on that reading list."

"I can't take that! That's a book your father gave you to get you ready for the college exams—"

"I know. But I want you to have it. I told him I planned to give it to you. He was anxious to meet you.... But now I don't think he can see anyone."

Zeb took the leather-bound book and held it in both hands, a priceless treasure. "Thank you," he said. He put it carefully on the table near the fireplace and picked up the book he had for Hannah. "Hannah, I want you to have my other blank book, so you can continue to write. I noticed you were getting close to the end of the one I gave you."

Hannah took it from him and held it against her chest. She walked into the bedroom and came out with something behind her back. "I've been trying to decide if I should tell you about this. Now I think you should know. You should understand what I did and why I did it."

"Understand what you did?"

She opened the book to the first page. "Listen," she said, and began to read aloud. *"I am glad that Zeb promised never to read this book unless I tell him he can. I doubt I ever will. I don't want him to know that on the first night we met, I stole his horse—"*

"You stole Christmas? But...but..." Zeb sputtered, "that's impossible! I would've awakened."

"When you've been with the outlaws for six months, you can tell when a man is sound asleep, especially if his mouth is wide open and he's snoring. Even with all that racket, you men don't wake up. The women are different...something to do with always listening for the babies."

She looked up at him shyly. "All I could think of after being with the outlaws was running away. So when you were asleep, I bunched up the blanket to make you think I was still there, then crept through the forest to Christmas. I couldn't mount him. He's too big. So I walked him until I found another tree lying on its side. I climbed on and rode him about an hour."

She took a deep breath. "Then I realized that without any money, I could never cross at the ferries. I couldn't buy any grain for the horse or any food for me. And if an outlaw saw me, I wouldn't have a chance. I turned around and brought him back, tied him to the limb, and came back into the clearing.

"I was still pretty sure you were just another outlaw," she continued. "You had two pistols and a rifle, and you were travelin' on the Natchez Road alone. I thought I'd ride with you until we crossed the Tennessee. Then I'd really steal your horse."

Zeb stared at her, astounded. "When did you decide I wasn't an outlaw? After we crossed the river?"

"No," she said. "It was before that." She turned to a page of the book. *"When I woke up the next morning, I was scared to death he would somehow know I took his horse. He would see that the horse was tied differently or something. Then he would just leave me in the forest. I lay there awake, watching him. He woke up and sat right up and started looking around. I got up and began to roll up the blanket. I wanted to be sure that he didn't think I was helpless.*

Three rings of mushrooms had sprouted overnight in the mossy area where I had been sitting. I saw him sort of glance over them and then suddenly his head turned and he was staring at the rings of mushrooms and then staring at me. I know what people say: that fairies dance at night in the forest and wherever they do, rings of mushrooms grow. Everybody says it, but I didn't think anyone really believed it.

He was looking at me, his eyes wide, his mouth open. I just said, "Maybe I am and maybe I ain't."

I decided he couldn't be an outlaw if he still believes in fairies dancing in the woods.

She closed the book and smiled up at Zeb.

He looked at the book. "Hannah's Diary," he said.

"It's just private thoughts and memories, some good, some funny, but some bad, too. Putting 'em down on paper helps me, somehow."

Zeb was reminded once again of the scared little girl he had met in the forest. She seemed so happy now. He hoped that, somehow, the bad memories she was recording would fade away.

He knew it was time for him to go.

Zeb stood and shook hands with Dr. McAllister. Hannah's mother hugged him and said quietly into his ear, "Thank you, Zeb. Thank you."

Nashoba threw his arms around Zeb. "As I told you once before, I am proud to call you 'brother.' When you come back,

I'll teach you how to play Ishtaboli and how to dance the Eagle Dance. I'll tell you what I've learned in school."

Zeb laughed "Thank you, Nashoba. I hope that one day I can return the favor."

Zeb held out his hand to Hannah. She stepped toward him and threw her arms around his waist, her wet, teary face pressed against his chest. "Zeb," she said, "I wish you were my brother."

He swallowed hard. "I guess after all we've been through, we're almost like brother and sister."

"Thank you for bringing me home."

Zeb looked down at the top of her head and smiled. Her hair had already grown back from the ragged mop she had when he found her. It was straight and black and fell almost to her shoulders now.

As he ran the back of his arm across his eyes, Hannah stepped back and looked up at him. Zeb picked up the book that Nashoba had given him.

"It's late," he said, "and the patrol will be leaving very early tomorrow morning. I will say good night and good-bye. Dr. and Mrs. McAllister, thank you for letting me be a part of your family."

He turned to Nashoba. "I will take care of this book and return it when I get back."

He put his hand on Hannah's shoulder. "Good-bye, Hannah."

Zeb turned, opened the door, and headed for his tent.

CHAPTER TWENTY-ONE

Homecoming

December 20, 1811

When Zeb arose the next morning, it seemed that the entire village of Yowani was already awake. He could smell the sweet aroma of breakfast yams and pigeons baking in the fire.

Zeb used the latrine and then washed his hands and face. The dragoons were already watering and feeding the horses to give them time to digest their food before the group started out. Zeb and Cracker Ryan fed and watered all seven of their horses. They tied them to the rail near the tents, ready to be tacked up for the journey north.

They joined the soldiers and ate a quick breakfast with the Choctaw. The pigeons, baked in clay, were moist and tender. Zeb broke the clay shell and pulled at the meat, licking his fingers between each bite. He dug into the sweet potato, marveling at how the sweet of the potatoes and the salty flavor of the baked pigeons went well together. He had taken such things for granted in the past. Zeb licked the grease from his lips, savoring the taste.

The dragoons had already moved their horses out to the entrance to the village, and Zeb and his grampa got their horses ready, then loaded Kapucha with baskets. The four draft horses were tacked up with bridles and lead lines. Grampa led the way on Andy with Zeb following on Christmas as they moved the horses toward the Nashville Road.

At the entrance to the village stood a group of Choctaw women, their arms folded, their faces expressionless. Eight large pack baskets loaded with food were standing in front of them. The baskets were open at the top. Zeb could see yams and dried corn, a mixture of grains for the horses, and two baskets of roasted venison and rabbit from last night's feast.

The dragoon horses were already lined up near the entrance, tethered to the fence rail. Captain Morrison, the sergeant, and the men stood in front of the Miko. The captain bowed formally to the Miko, then turned and faced the villagers. "We thank you and the entire village for having us here and sharing your celebration with us," he said in a loud voice. Then he smiled at the women standing near the saddlebags. "And in particular, we thank all of the women of the village who must have stayed up all night preparing these bags."

The Miko swept his arm toward the trail. "We hope that this will make it possible for you to travel north through Chickasaw country without having to hunt on their lands."

Captain Morrison moved over to where Cracker Ryan was standing with Zeb.

"Mr. Ryan," he said, "the army is in serious need of transport. We want to rent those four draft horses of yours to carry army provisions from here for as long as the provisions last, probably to just this side of Franklin. What would be your charge for that service?"

Zeb's grampa replied, "I would consider it my patriotic duty, sir. There will be no charge."

The captain bowed his head slightly. "Excellent!" he said. "I will give you a document to sign later." He then nodded to the sergeant. The soldiers lifted the baskets and placed them on the backs of the four draft horses. The baskets were connected in pairs, with straps and sheepskin pads so each horse could comfortably carry a basket on each side.

Zeb heard a high-pitched whistle. He grinned. *Only Hannah can whistle like that.* They had said their good-byes last night. Now Hannah signaled him in the gray dawn.

I've promised to come back, and Hannah knows I've never told her anything but the truth. That's why she trusts me. But when will I be able to keep that promise?

This time the sergeant organized the order of march. The sergeant and three of the mounted dragoons led the convoy. Behind them rode Cracker Ryan and Captain Morrison.

Zeb followed on Christmas, with Kapucha on lead.

Behind them rode four dragoons, each one leading a pack horse, and at the rear rode two more dragoons with guns at the ready.

Captain Morrison nodded to the sergeant, who raised his hand and shouted, "Move out!"

Except for short stops to water and feed the horses, and once for the men to eat pieces of the venison, they kept moving, always at a trot. By late afternoon, they had passed through Pigeon Roost. They stopped to camp at Line Creek, where Zeb and Hannah had first come across the army patrol. Captain Morrison estimated that they had covered nearly thirty-five miles that day. "It won't be this easy every day," he said.

Zeb wondered what he meant when he said "easy." That quick trot might be favored by the army, but it was sure hard on the rider. And he was glad that he had worked the big draft horses every day. He doubted they could take this pace otherwise.

Zeb groaned as he lifted the saddle from Christmas. The big horse took a deep breath and exhaled, relieved to have the load lightened and the tight girth gone. Zeb untied the rolled-up tent and retrieved his blanket roll and the saddlebags from Kapucha. He put up the tent, then kneeled at the entrance flaps to spread the ground cloth and set his bedroll inside.

As he backed out of the tent, he bumped into his grampa. "Zeb," his grampa said, "Captain Morrison thinks that the army is goin' to want a lot of horses in a hurry, maybe before the next year is out."

"But we won't have any ready—"

"That's the point. I've been workin' on a plan ever since I bought Christmas. But it's late and I want to think more about it. We can talk about it tomorrow as we travel up the trail."

Zeb stretched out on his bed and pulled the blanket around him. He looked up at the canvas ceiling of the tent, softly lit by the waning moon.

Zeb and his grampa awoke to the sound of heavy rain. They grinned when they realized the inside of the tent was dry.

They joined the army mess and shared the food that the Choctaw had given them, thankful that they didn't have to try to cook in the downpour. The cold venison tasted stronger than it had the night before. The group mounted and rode all day. Zeb and his grampa each used half of their new tent as a poncho, but it didn't make any real difference. They were soon soaked to the skin by blowing rain.

The second night after leaving Yowani when they stopped to camp, Zeb sat near the cook fire to hear his grampa's idea. "The army is goin' to need a lot of horses," the old man said. "It's no secret. Our country is havin' a lot of problems with the English. They've sent troops up to Canada, and they have troops and ships down in Pensacola. They're takin' Americans off ships on the high seas. For them, the Revolutionary War of Independence was never really over."

"But Grampa, if they're gonna need a lot of horses this comin' year, we won't have any ready to sell. Even if Mama and Josh were able to get back most of those year-old colts, we couldn't—"

"You're right," his grampa said.

"So what'll we do?"

"We can go up to the Lexington area and buy their culls."

"Their culls!"

"That's what Christmas was. I'm not talkin' about culls in the usual sense. Those breeders up there are raisin' horses mainly for horse racing. After a year, two at the most, if the horse doesn't show any promise, they try to sell 'em as saddle horses."

"I doubt they'd make good saddle horses without a lot of training. Wrong temperament. They haven't been trained for that. They're used to runnin' full out."

"Exactly!" his grampa exclaimed. "And for that reason, they never get much money for 'em. And if they can't sell 'em, they put 'em down."

"So?"

"I think we should go up to Lexington and look over the culls from the various breeders. Pick out suitable ones, offer a low but reasonable price, which is better than nothing, bring them back to the farm, and retrain them for the army!"

"We'd hafta start right away—" Zeb stopped as another aftershock shook the ground.

He and his grampa moved out to the center of the meadow away from the trees. When the temblor was over, they checked the seven horses. They had already calmed down. *I wonder if the earthquake was felt up in Franklin. We're getting mighty close, and we're still feeling the aftershocks. I hope no one was hurt.* Zeb sighed. *Six more days to go.*

The convoy continued to feel aftershocks from the quake.

Captain Morrison had warned them all, "As you ride, check the trees as well as the road. If you see one tree leaning against another, be prepared to get out of its way. You dragoons, break ranks, but get out of the way!"

The group struggled to travel at least thirty miles a day, and Zeb was worried about the big draft horses. Although Zeb and Lonnie Champ had worked them hard for over a month back at Culpepper's place, trying to get them into condition for the long trip, they were already showing signs of not being able to keep up with the army's pace.

As the convoy traveled on the Nashville Road, Chickasaw braves sometimes appeared out of the forest and watched them pass. At night, when the group had set up camp, a few of the older braves approached, seeming friendly. They told the dragoons how many sleeps it was to the next big water and warned them about dangerous bogs. Zeb felt that the Chickasaw simply wanted them to keep moving.

In the group of Chickasaw watching them, there were often two or three braves about Zeb's age. Sometimes they would stand at the forest's edge and watch the men setting up camp. The next evening, after a long and tiring ride, Zeb unsaddled Christmas and tethered him in a small patch of grass. He was starting to put up his tent when some young braves suddenly appeared at his side.

One of them pointed at Zeb's little Spanish army shovel, still hanging on the saddle. Zeb untied the thongs and showed it to him. The brave passed it to the others and then handed it back. They didn't seem to know what it was for.

Zeb finished putting up the tent, then dug a trench around it with the little shovel. The brave who had shown so much interest put out his hand. Zeb handed him the shovel. The young man studied it, running his fingers along the edge. He knelt down and dug into the dirt. He stood and smiled at the others, then ran into the forest with the shovel held above his head.

The other braves burst into laughter. Without thinking, Zeb, suddenly furious, ran after him. The brave he was chasing continued to laugh as he ran through the thick woods.

The laughter reminded Zeb of what Nashoba had told him. For the Choctaw and the Chickasaw, there is no private property. Among the youth, if someone has something you like, you grab it and run. If he catches you, you give it back. No one thinks any less of you for taking it.

The young brave stumbled, and Zeb leaped on him, knocking him to the ground. They wrestled for a moment, the shovel thrown to one side, forgotten. *This is like wrestling with Nashoba,* Zeb thought, *but Nashoba is older and stronger and always wins.* In this case Zeb was stronger and maybe a year older. The young brave suddenly relaxed and grinned up at him. Zeb got to his feet and offered his hand to the brave to help him up. The brave picked up the shovel and offered it to Zeb. They returned to the camp side by side.

Captain Morrison met them as they approached the camp-site. Cracker Ryan was standing behind him, glowering and slapping his coiled whip against his thigh. Captain Morrison spoke to Zeb in a low, angry voice. "That was very dangerous and foolish, Zeb. I couldn't send one of the soldiers after you. We are committed to maintaining peace with the Chickasaw."

"I admit I went after him without thinking. But it's all a game, Captain Morrison. I learned that from Nashoba and the other Choctaw. There are no hard feelings."

Captain Morrison looked at Zeb and the Chickasaw brave standing next to him. They were both smiling. The young Chickasaw had his hand on Zeb's shoulder.

"It wasn't as much of a game as you may think, Zeb. Four of those young braves started after you two. One of them had pulled a stone hatchet from his belt. Your grandfather snapped that whip of his and held up his hand. The message was clear. 'Let the two of them work it out.'"

Zeb stared at the faces of the other braves. They were not smiling.

Captain Morrison locked his eyes with Zeb's. "Remember, the Chickasaw and the Choctaw are very different. It worked out this time, Zeb," Captain Morrison continued. "I want you to know, however, if something like this happens again, I will not make any hostile move against the Chickasaw. You will be completely on your own."

Before Zeb had time to think over what had just occurred, the earth began to shake again. The convoy automatically moved away from leaners and waited for the shaking to stop. The oldest of the Chickasaw braves motioned to Captain Morrison, pointing at the ground in confusion. Captain Morrison shrugged, his hands open. "I don't know," he said, shaking his head. *I wonder if they understand what a shrug means,* Zeb thought. *Can they tell he is trying to tell them we don't know what causes it either?*

The next morning, they started out early. The young Chickasaw were still with them. The group crossed creeks and slogged through bogs.

The braves finally disappeared when the patrol reached an army road-clearing crew. They were cutting down leaners and moving fallen trees off the road. In one area the army had placed logs crossways on the trail to try to make some of the wet lowlands passable.

They crossed the Tennessee River on the Colbert Ferry. It cost Zeb fifty cents for each horse and fifty cents for his grampa and himself. He remembered when he had angrily called the Colbert brothers "typical half-breeds," charging the poor travelers high prices. He hated thinking about how that comment hurt Hannah's feelings. Now, he was glad to pay and keep moving toward home.

Three days later, the convoy crossed the Duck River at the Gordon Ferry. *Are the ferrymen still keeping their eyes open for "a shaggy-haired boy riding a big horse," as Tate McPhee's men had asked them to?* Zeb wondered.

It was dark when they set up camp near Joslin's Stand. Zeb wished they could go on. *Only two hours and we're home,* he thought. Grampa was still riding well, but he was obviously very tired. Sometimes he rode bent over, half asleep.

The draft horses had become more and more strained. Captain Morrison had slowed the pace a bit and ordered more stops, but the horses were still having a hard time keeping up.

As the dragoons, Zeb, and his grampa set up camp, they could hear a horse galloping in their direction. The soldier on guard stood in the middle of the Nashville Road with his rifle at the ready, but the guard relaxed when he saw that it was the post rider.

The post rider rode up to Captain Morrison and saluted. "I borrowed a fresh horse from the clearing crew. They said you were just ahead. I had orders to reach you before you deliver your letter to Mr. Andrew Jackson."

Captain Morrison asked the rider to dismount. The man did so, then opened the saddlebag and took out several letters. He handed two of them to Captain Morrison and then leaned, exhausted, against the horse. "Your commanding officer asked me to tell you that he would like you to read the one addressed to you immediately."

While Captain Morrison was reading the letter, the post rider asked, "Is Cracker Ryan with you?"

Captain Morrison pointed to where Zeb's grampa was standing, then continued reading his letter. Cracker Ryan moved over to the post rider. "You looked exhausted, Bobby. Come and sit down. We'll give you something to eat."

"I have a letter for you," he said as Zeb's grampa led him toward the campfire.

Captain Morrison called the dragoons together near where Cracker Ryan, Zeb, and the post rider were sitting. "Let me share some news with you." He began to read aloud from the letter. *"We think the earthquake was centered near New Madrid. The damage at New Madrid reported to Fort Dearborn by flat-boat crews was catastrophic! Every building in New Madrid was flattened. Most of the inhabitants were killed."*

"Grampa," Zeb asked, his heart pounding, "isn't that where Tate McPhee and his gang went?"

The old man nodded.

Captain Morrison continued. *"The damage in Washington was minimal. A huge crevasse opened up and swallowed a house and barn, but no one was killed as far as we know."*

"Thank God," Zeb said.

"Please take notice: Dancey Moore escaped from the stockade at Fort Dearborn with the help of ex-sergeant Michael Scruggs. They have either gone south to New Orleans or are headed north up the Nashville Road. We expect them to join an outlaw gang. I am alerting you to this problem since they may be coming your way."

That night, extra guards were put on sentry duty.

As Zeb and his grampa walked away from the campfire that evening, Zeb looked up at the night sky.

"Grampa," he said, "the first night I came to Natchez looking for you, I saw the comet sitting up there in the sky like a ball of fire with two tails behind it."

"I saw it, too," his grampa said. "It was something, wasn't it?"

Zeb thought for a moment. "Some people said it was a bad omen, that it was a sign we were coming into bad times. Do you think that's true?"

"No, Zeb. I think things are starting to look up for us. Just think, you got Hannah home, you found me, we got Andy and Christmas back, and now we're almost home." His grampa bent down to crawl inside the tent.

"Wait, Grampa. Didn't the post rider bring you a letter today? What did it say?"

"It was for both of us. Here, you can read it."

Zeb crawled out of the tent and sat on one of the logs near the campfire. He opened the letter.

Dear Cracker and Zeb:

I hope that this finds you in good health and almost home. Cracker, I have been thinking about your idea regarding the training of culls. We have a number of people trying to breed racehorses here. Many of their foals will never do for racing and most of them are not much good for anything else. The temperament is all wrong. I have seen a few here that have possibilities, but it would take a lot of patience and skill to retrain them. Katie could probably do some of it, but it would take someone like Zeb to make it work. Let me know. If you like the idea, I have four horses in mind already.

Best regards,
John Culpepper

Zeb crawled back into the tent, where his grampa was snoring softly. He smiled, thinking of home. He looked forward to working on the horse farm with his grampa again. He thought of his mama and how much pain he had caused her. Would she have baked one of those loaves of bread? His stomach growled. He could almost smell it. He closed his eyes. *We're almost home.*

The next morning Zeb checked the packs on each of the draft horses. The Choctaw food baskets were empty now. He tacked up Christmas and was ready to go before the patrol had finished breakfast. But it was still too dark to leave.

Zeb's grampa crawled out of the tent, smiled, and stood watching Zeb. "Getting a little anxious, Zeb?"

"Yes, sir, I guess I am. The draft horses are ready to go. Once we get the horses tacked up and our tents and bedrolls tied up, we can leave any time."

They moved out of the camp with the first light. When they reached the upper meadow of the Ryan horse farm, the dragoons handed Zeb the leads for each of the four horses the army had borrowed. The army patrol left and hurried on to Nashville.

Zeb and his grampa sat on their horses, the draft horses gathered around them on their leads, and looked down into the valley below. In the distance they could see the farmhouse, almost hidden by the pine trees Zeb's grampa had planted thirty years earlier. A wisp of white smoke rose lazily from the cookstove chimney.

They could see Josh loading up his arms with firewood. As he turned to go back into the house, he looked up and spotted them. He waved and then danced around in the dirt yard. He dropped the firewood and raced into the farmhouse.

Zeb's grampa started to zigzag down the steep grassy meadow, leading two of the draft horses. Zeb paused for a moment, staring down into the valley below. Then he urged Christmas forward, leading Kapucha and the other two draft horses behind him.

Author's Note

Were there really an earthquake and a comet in the year 1811?

Yes, and more wonders. The people of the Mississippi Territory called 1811 "The Year of Wonders." On March 25, 1811, Flaugergues Honoré discovered a comet, which appeared low in the western sky. It had two tails, which astronomers today have estimated to be 132 million miles long. The comet was visible off and on for about nine months, increasing in brightness during September and October 1811, the period when Zeb and Hannah were in Natchez. Many people thought that the comet was a bad omen, warning them that something terrible was about to happen.

Something bad did happen, but the comet had nothing to do with this second wonder. On December 16, 1811, at two o'clock in the morning, the southeastern United States was hit with the worst earthquake ever recorded in America. It was centered in New Madrid, Missouri, and totally destroyed that small city. The quake was so powerful that it changed the course of the Mississippi River in many places and created Reelfoot Lake in western Tennessee. For a short while, the river ran backward—upstream—as the lake filled up. The earthquake was so strong that the shaking ground rang church bells in Virginia and even the Liberty Bell in Philadelphia, Pennsylvania, about 800 miles away. It was felt across the nation, almost to the Rocky Mountains. Strong aftershocks continued through December 1811, and tremors were still being felt in early February 1812.

The earthquake was actually three earthquakes occurring very close together. Geologists now believe that the three earthquakes were each of a magnitude of 8.0 or higher on the Richter scale, almost as strong as the San Francisco earthquake of 1906 (magnitude of 8.25). The three New Madrid earthquakes are among the great quakes of recent history, changing the face of North America—with large areas sunk into the earth, new lakes formed, and forests destroyed—more than any earthquake ever on the continent.

The third wonder of 1811 was the steamboat *New Orleans*. Built in Pittsburgh, Pennsylvania, by Nicholas Roosevelt and Robert Fulton, it was launched on the Ohio River in Pittsburgh in September 1811. It stopped in St. Louis and, to the amazement of bystanders and possible investors, the steamboat demonstrated that it could steam upstream! The *New Orleans* was in the Mississippi River when the earthquake hit and, although the steamboat was not severely damaged, the captain had great difficulty navigating the river for many weeks, as known channels had disappeared and new, unknown channels had formed.

The *New Orleans* demonstrated once again that it could steam upstream when it reached Natchez in late December 1811. Hannah and Zeb just missed seeing it. Shortly after its arrival in the city of New Orleans on January 10, 1812, the boat began regular service between New Orleans and Natchez.

The steamboat *New Orleans* sank a few years later when it hit a log which pierced the hull.

How did the steam paddleboat change life in the Mississippi Territory, in Natchez, and along the Natchez Trace? How did it affect the Choctaw?

In 1814, two years after the steamboat New Orleans reached New Orleans, there were twenty-one steamboat arrivals in that city. The impact on the economy of Natchez was enormous. It was now possible to ship huge quantities of bailed cotton to New Orleans by steamboat, then ship them to the mills in Liverpool, England, and in Boston. Cotton became king.

Many slave owners in the Mississippi Territory had manumitted their slaves, or set them free. But cotton was a labor-intensive crop, and the demand for slaves increased sharply with the economic boom of cotton. Laws were passed in 1840 making the manumission of slaves illegal.

The economic prosperity in Mississippi attracted many white settlers to the region. Their demand for land in the Mississippi Territory put pressure on the U. S. government, which eventually led to the infamous Treaty of Dancing Rabbit Creek and the removal of the Choctaw from Mississippi, forcing them to join other Indians already being driven out on the Trail of Tears.

Regular upstream steamboat traffic to St. Louis and to Pittsburgh changed the nature of the Natchez Road. The rich merchants who owned the flatboats—used in the Mississippi and its tributaries through the late 1800s—returned north on steamboats, so the only victims left for outlaws on the Road were the flatboat men walking with little money. The outlaws disappeared from the forest.

Why did the U. S. Army call the cavalry the Mounted Light Dragoons?

During the late sixteenth century, the armies of Europe attacked on horseback. It was nearly impossible to fire a musket accurately while mounted, so a special flintlock musket with a short barrel and a pistol handle was invented. The musket evolved into a pistol, and the hammer of the flintlock mechanism on the new pistol was shaped like a dragon. Soon the pistol itself was called a dragoon (possibly a mispronunciation of "dragon"). Later the name was applied to the troops as well.

The dragoons in Europe and in the United States were considered part of the infantry. They attacked on horseback but carried out defense on foot, as it would have been impossible to load and reload the one-shot muskets or the pistols while mounted.

What was the strange sand that Zeb encountered in Natchez Under-the-Hill?

The light, grainy sand is called "loess." It is topsoil that had blown off the western grasslands thousands of years earlier, during the Ice Age, and deposited in a thick layer along the Mississippi River. It is a mixture of fine sand and organic material.